Sadie Rose
AND THE PHANTOM WARRIOR

A PRAIRIE FAMILY ADVENTURE

Sadie Rose
AND THE
PHANTOM WARRIOR

Hilda Stahl

CROSSWAY BOOKS • WHEATON, ILLINOIS
A DIVISION OF GOOD NEWS PUBLISHERS

Sadie Rose and the Phantom Warrior.

Copyright © 1991 by Hilda Stahl.

Published by Crossway Books, a division of
Good News Publishers, Wheaton, Illinois 60187.

Cover illustration: Kathy Kulin

First printing, 1991

Printed in the United States of America

Library of Congress Cataloging-in-Publication Data
Stahl, Hilda.
   Sadie Rose and the phantom warrior / Hilda Stahl.
        p.   cm. — (A prairie family adventure)
   Summary: Out on the Nebraska prairie with her brother, Sadie
Rose sees an Indian warrior, runs into cousins from Michigan, and
searches for a missing friend.
   [1. Frontier and pioneer life—Fiction.   2. Indians—Fiction.
3. Christian life—Fiction.]   I. Title.   II. Series: Stahl, Hilda.
Prairie family adventure.
PZ7.S78244Sag   1991   [Fic]—dc20   90-24471
ISBN 0-89107-612-3

99		98		97		96		95		94		93		92		91
15	14	13	12	11	10	9	8	7	6	5	4	3	2	1

Dedicated with love to
Kim Bailey

Contents

1
The Ghost

Her faded sunbonnet hanging down her thin back, Sadie stood with Apple beside the creek in the shade of a giant cottonwood tree and looked downstream for Riley. He'd spotted an antelope and wanted to shoot it to take it home to the family. The huge red sun was peeking over a distant hill, and a warm Nebraska wind was blowing. Sadie had smothered the campfire and had strapped her saddlebag behind Apple's saddle. "Riley, you said you wouldn't be long," muttered Sadie.

Suddenly the short hairs at the back of Sadie's neck under her braids stood on end, and a chill ran down her spine. Apple bobbed her head and moved restlessly. Slowly Sadie turned. On the side of a low hill in the tall grass stood a big bronze, bare-chested Indian dressed in blue U.S. cavalry pants. A black lock of hair stood up like a horn on his otherwise bald head. Silver bands circled his muscled arms. His face was blackened and streaked with red and white paint. He was looking right at her!

"Riley!" Sadie whispered frantically through a bone-dry throat.

The Indian took a step toward her. Fear pricked her skin, and for a minute she thought she'd faint dead away, something she'd never done in all her twelve years.

Just then she heard hoofbeats coming along the creek behind her. Was it Riley or another Indian? Sadie wanted to turn and shout for Riley or even run, but she couldn't move.

Against her will Sadie glanced over her shoulder, then quickly back, and in that instant the Indian had disappeared. Her thin legs trembled inside bibbed overalls that once had belonged to Riley. He'd outgrown them before they'd moved from Douglas County to live at the edge of the sandhills on the Circle Y Ranch. Apple nickered a greeting, and Sadie knew Riley had ridden up on Caleb's mare, Bay.

"What're you looking at, Sadie?" asked Riley from behind her. He was sixteen and full-grown, with the muscles of a man.

"Get down, Riley!" she hissed as she dropped to the ground and crawled around the base of the cottonwood to put it between her and the Indian. Blood pounded in her ears. Would they both be scalped before they could get back to the Circle Y? They'd left a few days ago to track down the Malda family and return two of their children to them and get back Riley's colt, Lasso. Last night, when it had grown too dark on the Nebraska prairie to see, Riley had finally agreed to camp.

Riley dropped from Bay and crouched beside

Sadie, the rifle clutched in his hand. "What's wrong?" he whispered.

"An Indian warrior!" she whispered hoarsely.

"Oh, Sadie," said Riley with a laugh as he jumped up beside the big bay mare. "You're sure bein' silly."

Sadie stared at him, then grabbed his hand and tried to pull him back down behind the tree. "We'll be scalped!" She'd heard and read stories about raiding parties.

"Sadie, there aren't any wild Indians in Nebraska any more. They were all put on reservations a few years ago."

"Lost Sand Cherry is an Indian, and she's living at Joshua Cass's ranch!"

"But she's his wife! What is wrong with you, Sadie Rose York?"

Frantically Sadie looked out across the vast rolling hills. The bright sky stretched on and on to sit like an upside-down blue bowl on the green grass. The only trees in sight were the few along the creek. The Indian was gone! Finally Sadie turned back to Riley, her brown eyes large in her white face. "I did see an Indian! . . . With war paint on his face! He stood right over there!" She pointed to the side of the hill.

"Sadie, it was only your imagination." Riley glanced quickly around, not expecting to see anything but the usual birds and other wildlife that roamed the prairie. "You've had too much excitement the last few days."

"He was real!"

"Maybe it was a ghost," said Riley with a chuckle as he pushed his rifle into the boot of his saddle.

"He was real, Riley Merrill York!"

"Maybe a phantom," said Riley, laughing harder as he adjusted the bedroll behind his saddle. He figured Sadie probably didn't know that ghost and phantom were the same thing. He had to admit that she was acting like she had seen an Indian warrior, but he knew she couldn't have. She could tease as well as the rest of the family, but this was more than he'd expected from her. "No more jokes, Sadie. Let's get going so we'll have time to stop to see Lost Sand Cherry."

"And Levi," said Sadie sharply. She knew Riley didn't like Levi even though they were the same age. Levi had always been a rancher and had never had to use a plow like Riley had on the farm back in Douglas County before Pa had died in the terrible blizzard. Now with Momma married to Caleb York, Riley was a rancher and wore slanted high-heeled boots, tough denim pants, and a wide-brimmed hat. He sat tall and proud in the saddle just like Caleb York.

Riley smiled, his white teeth flashing in his sun-browned face. "I'm not mad at Levi any longer. Not even for being mean to us when we found out his pa was married to an Indian." Riley swung easily into the saddle. "I like Lost Sand Cherry. Levi shouldn't be ashamed to have her for a mother."

Sadie knew Riley was trying to get her mind off the Indian warrior, but it wasn't working. She grabbed the saddle horn and struggled up into the saddle. Apple was shorter than Bay, but still too tall for Sadie to mount easily. She hated to be short. She had grown some in the past month, but not enough to be as tall as her fifteen-year-old sister, Opal. Sadie's shoes no longer fit her, so she was wearing Opal's until Caleb had enough cash money to buy her new ones.

Shivering, Sadie followed Riley off across the hills toward the Cass ranch. She saw a movement to her left and jumped so hard that daylight showed between her and the saddle. Was it the Indian warrior? The dirty yellow back and tail of a coyote bobbed up and down in the tall grass, and Sadie breathed easier.

"I'm telling Lost Sand Cherry about that Indian," said Sadie with her chin high and her dark eyes flashing. She knew by the shape of the hills that they were almost at the Cass ranch. Warm wind ruffled the wide sleeves of the shirt she wore that once had been Riley's.

Riley pushed his wide-brimmed hat to the back of his dark head. "She'll laugh at you just like I did."

Sadie shrugged. "Maybe Levi and Lost Sand Cherry saw the Indian."

Riley frowned. "Sadie, you're carrying this too far."

"You'll believe me when *you* see him! I just hope it's not too late!"

Suddenly a scream pierced the air.

Sadie's blood ran cold. Had the Indian scalped Lost Sand Cherry?

Riley leaned low in the saddle and urged Bay toward the scream.

Sadie hesitated a second, then sped after Riley, her brown braids whipping around her face and shoulders. She wanted to cry out for Riley to stop before he ran into danger, but she couldn't force any words past the hard lump in her throat or the rush of wind against her face.

Riley and Sadie rode into the valley where the Cass ranch sprawled. They saw a girl about Opal's size running toward them, her blue sunbonnet bobbing around her slender shoulders. Her black hair streamed out behind her, and her blue eyes looked wild with fear. She wore a new-looking blue and yellow calico dress that hung well below her knees, dark stockings, and black shoes. She spotted Riley and desperately waved her arms and shouted, "Help! Help!"

Riley dropped beside her, his rifle in his hand. She grabbed his arm, but couldn't speak for a minute. Riley looked for a sign of danger, but couldn't see anything. "What's wrong?" he asked.

The girl cried harder and pointed behind her.

Sadie looked frantically around for the Indian warrior. A sod barn stood beside a stream with two massive cottonwoods shading the corral, the sod chicken coop, and the yard. Across the long yard a small frame house was built close to a hill for protection from winter wind and snow. There was no sign of the warrior. Sadie leaped from the saddle and stood beside Riley and the girl, then looked toward the house. Why didn't Lost Sand Cherry or Levi come out? Sadie knew Joshua Cass would be gone on business a couple more days. "What's the matter?" Sadie asked the girl sharply.

"Indian!" the girl finally blurted out, pointing to the house.

Sadie gasped. "Is the Indian in the house?"

"Yes!" cried the girl, clinging to Riley with both hands. "With Ma and the baby!"

Riley frowned down at the girl. Was she seeing things too?

"Did he have on war paint and was he tall?" asked Sadie hoarsely.

The girl stared at Sadie for a long time. "I never saw an Indian man. It was a woman. She walked right out of that house, and Ma and the baby

14

walked right in with her. I tried to stop Ma, but she wouldn't listen to me." The girl burst into wild tears. "They're probably already dead! I wanted to go in and check, but I just couldn't do it." She gingerly touched her long, flowing hair. "I don't want to be scalped."

Riley pried the girl's fingers loose and pushed her at Sadie. "Talk some sense into her while I go talk to Lost Sand Cherry."

As Riley strode toward the small frame house, Sadie gripped the girl's thin arm. "The woman you saw is our friend. She wouldn't hurt anyone. She wouldn't scalp your ma or the baby."

The girl rubbed her eyes, leaving a streak of dirt across her rosy cheek. "Are you sure?"

"I'm sure. But . . . did you see a warrior?"

"No." The girl looked around fearfully. "Did we come to Nebraska to get killed? I want to go home!"

"You won't get killed." Sadie trembled as she pictured the Indian she'd seen. Maybe they would all be killed! "Let's go wait in the shade of the trees." Leading Apple, Sadie walked the girl to the edge of the stream as Riley went into the house. Apple drank while Sadie turned to the girl. "I'm Sadie York. Who're are you?"

The girl took a deep breath as she looked toward the house, then back at Sadie. "I'm Gerda Tasker. Are you sure that Indian won't hurt my ma?"

"I'm sure."

Just then Riley stepped out on the porch, waved, and called, "Come here, Sadie. Bring the girl."

Gerda hung back. "I won't go in the same house with an Indian!"

Sadie sighed heavily. "My brother Riley said to take you in, so I gotta."

"Oh, all right. But if that Indian even tries to touch me, I'll scream my head off."

Sadie rolled her eyes and walked toward the house. Just as she reached the porch she glanced back and saw a movement at the back corner of the barn. Was it the painted Indian? Or had she only imagined him, just as Gerda had imagined Lost Sand Cherry would scalp them all?

2
Bad News

Before he opened the door again Riley turned to Sadie and whispered, "Don't say a word about the Indian brave you think you saw."

Sadie frowned, but didn't argue. It wouldn't do any good to try to convince Riley she wasn't teasing. He wouldn't believe she'd seen the warrior until he saw the man himself.

"Are you sure we shouldn't run and hide?" whispered Gerda, stopping short of the door.

Riley shot Gerda an impatient look and opened the door.

Lost Sand Cherry stood just inside. She wore the calico dress of the white woman, but a Pawnee band around her forehead and beaded moccasins. A baby's cry pierced the air. "Sadie, I am thankful to God you and Riley stopped." She looked past them at Gerda. "You are daughter to Essie Tasker."

17

Gerda ran to a woman sitting in the rocking chair with a baby at her breast. "Ma, you didn't get scalped!" cried Gerda.

"Hush, child," said the woman with a slight frown.

Sadie shot a look at Lost Sand Cherry, but the expression on her face didn't change. Maybe she was used to people thinking she'd scalp them.

"Essie Tasker, this is Caleb York's girl, Sadie," said Lost Sand Cherry.

Essie had circles under her dark eyes. Brown hair straggled out from the bun at the back of her head. Her brown dress was streaked with dirt. "Glad to meet you," said Essie with a faint smile. She was too occupied with quieting the baby and listening to Gerda's whispers to hear Riley and Sadie's response. "These are my children . . . Joey and Gerda. Joey doesn't feel well."

"I could hold him a while to let you rest," said Sadie.

Gerda frowned. "Ma can take care of Joey herself."

Sadie flushed and turned back to Lost Sand Cherry.

Just then Joey stopped crying, and Essie said, "Is your momma Bess Merrill?"

Sadie and Riley turned to Essie in surprise. "Yes," they said at the same time. "Bess York now," said Riley.

"I'm her cousin from Michigan," said Essie.

Gerda gasped. "These kids are cousins to us?"

"Must be," said Essie.

Sadie stared at Riley, then at Essie and Gerda. Cousins?

Riley couldn't stand the thought of having Gerda as a cousin. But he knew it wouldn't be right to say so. "Momma will be glad to see family from Michigan," he finally said.

Sadie nodded. Momma asked everyone that stopped by the ranch if they were from Michigan. So far nobody had been. And now when they did meet someone from Michigan, it had to be a girl Sadie didn't like at all!

"We're going to see your momma as soon as Mart gets back from Jake's Crossing," said Essie. The baby started crying again, and she turned her attention back to him.

"Where's Levi?" Riley asked Lost Sand Cherry with a quick glance around.

A great sadness filled her dark eyes. "He and his mare Netty have been gone since you were here with the two Malda children a few days ago. I am very worried."

"But where would he go?" asked Sadie. She liked Levi Cass, and once she'd even let herself think she could fall in love with him if she was old enough.

"I don't know." Lost Sand Cherry shook her head. "He is very angry you two learned that I am married to his pa. But he promised Joshua before he left that he'd stay to tend to chores. Levi would not break a promise even if he was angry and embarrassed."

Sadie shivered. Maybe a wolf had attacked him. Or maybe the wild Indian had killed him and scalped him.

"I'll go look for him," said Riley.

"I'll go with you," said Sadie. She didn't want Riley out on the vast prairie alone with the Indian warrior. She knew he was real, and she intended to keep a sharp eye out for him.

"I want to go too!" cried Gerda, running to stand with them.

"You'd be in the way. You can't go," said Essie Tasker, rocking the baby to stop his crying.

"Ma! I want to go! I do! I do!" Gerda stamped her foot and stuck her lip out in a pout.

Sadie and Riley stared at her in shock. They would never dare talk back to Momma, nor would they stamp a foot or pout.

"Your pa will be coming back, and he'll want to leave right away," said Essie weakly.

"He can just wait!" cried Gerda with a flip of her long, flowing hair. "He made us wait here last night and this morning! I am going with them!"

Riley wanted to tell Gerda he wouldn't take her along no matter what, but he knew he couldn't be so rude.

Sadie bit her tongue to keep from telling Gerda to obey her mother.

"It would be better if you didn't go with them," said Lost Sand Cherry. "They know the prairie and you don't."

Gerda glared at Lost Sand Cherry. "No Indian can tell me what to do. I will go." Gerda caught Riley's arm and pulled hard. "Come on, let's go."

"Now, Gerda . . ." said Essie.

"Ma!"

Essie sighed heavily. "Have it your way. You always do."

Riley pulled free of Gerda and walked out the door to Bay.

Sadie said, "Good-bye, Lost Sand Cherry. We'll find Levi."

"God go with you," said Lost Sandy Cherry.

Sadie smiled and ran to Apple.

"Where do I ride?" asked Gerda, following Sadie.

Riley frowned. "We only have two horses." He was sure she'd stay behind once he pointed that out.

"I'll ride with Sadie," said Gerda.

Sadie sat in the saddle and looked down at Gerda. "Do you know how to ride a horse?"

"No, but there can't be much to learn." Gerda reached up to Sadie. "Pull me up and I'll ride behind you."

Sadie looked helplessly at Riley, and he finally shrugged. They both had been taught to be nice. They knew Jesus wanted them to be kind, but oh, it was hard with Gerda! Sadie gripped Gerda's hand and helped her up behind her. Gerda's dress hiked up, showing her legs where her stockings ended just above her shoes. Sadie flushed with embarrassment, but Gerda didn't seem to care if Riley saw her leg almost to her knee. Sadie would never let a boy see her bare legs. She was glad she wore Riley's old overalls and shirt.

"We'll check where they pasture their cattle," said Riley, turning Bay toward the south. The sun was already hot in the sky even though it was still morning. He'd been to the Cass ranch with Caleb York twice already, and he knew where the south pasture was.

"Hold on tight, Gerda," said Sadie as she nudged Apple to follow Bay.

Gerda squealed and clung to the back straps of Sadie's overalls. "Be careful! I almost fell off!"

Sadie wanted to stop Apple and send Gerda back to the house, but she followed Riley around the edge of a couple of sandhills to a fenced-in area. A windmill squawked in the warm wind. Cattle milled around the huge wooden tank. Smells of dusty cattle and fresh manure were strong in the air. Sadie looked around for the Indian, but all she saw was the blowing prairie grass and several birds flying across the wide sky.

"I want a drink," said Gerda.

"My canteen is tied beside your leg," said Sadie.

"I want a drink of that cold water running from that pipe," said Gerda, pointing toward the tank.

"Riley, Gerda wants a drink," called Sadie.

Riley turned in the saddle with a frown. "It doesn't look like anyone rode through the fence in a good while. We'll ride the fence line to look for Levi."

"We're not goin' inside the pasture," said Sadie in case Gerda didn't understand what Riley was saying. "Drink from the canteen."

"I will not!" cried Gerda, tugging hard on Sadie's overalls. "I want a cold drink!"

Riley heard Gerda, and his temper shot sky-high. He rode back to Apple and looked Gerda in the eye. "You can get off right here and get your drink, but we're riding the fence line to find Levi. You can stay here at the windmill or you can come with us, but you can't do both."

Gerda gasped. No one had ever talked to her that way before. She was afraid to stay at the windmill with all the wild cattle, so she tossed her head and said, "I'll stay with you."

Sadie bit back a grin. She was glad Riley had taken a firm stand with Gerda.

Several feet away a jack rabbit stood tall, looked around, then bounded away in mighty leaps. A hawk cried in the bright blue sky. Sadie didn't see any sign of the Indian warrior. Was it possible she had imagined him? She frowned. No, he was real!

Riley studied the ground carefully as he rode along. He couldn't track like Joshua or Levi Cass, but he was learning. After several minutes of careful looking he spotted a set of hoofprints. He knew they couldn't be too old since it had rained a few nights ago. The tracks led away from the fence, so he followed them. They were small and could easily be Netty's tracks. Netty and Apple were about the same size. Bay's hoofprints were bigger.

From time to time Riley glanced back the way they'd come. Caleb had told him how important it was to pay close attention to where he'd come from so he wouldn't get lost going back. Riley studied the shape of the hills and the position of the blowouts too. Where grass didn't grow on a sandy hill, the strong wind blew the side of the hill right away, making a blowout. Sometimes the whole top of the hill was blown away, leaving a deep hole. Riley knew never to ride over a hill unless he checked it carefully.

From the corner of her eye Sadie saw a movement. Her heart dropped to her feet. Was it the Indian? She turned her head and studied the prairie, but didn't see anything. Maybe it had been a coyote . . . or her vivid imagination.

"What're you looking at?" asked Gerda nervously.

Sadie shrugged. She knew Riley wouldn't want her to tell Gerda about the Indian. For a minute Sadie wanted to anyway, just to give Gerda a scare. Sadie clamped her mouth shut to keep from doing such an ornery thing.

"How come you won't talk to me?" asked Gerda.

23

"Riley wants us to be quiet."

"I sure don't have to do what he says!"

Sadie nudged Apple into a faster pace, and Gerda squealed in fright.

"You did that on purpose, didn't you!"

Sadie grinned, but didn't answer.

"You're not very nice. I wish I'd stayed with Ma."

Sadie wished so too.

Riley spotted a tree with a creek running along beside it. He rode toward it, then suddenly pulled up short.

Her heart racing, Sadie reined Apple in beside him. "What's wrong?" she whispered.

"I thought I heard a shot."

"A gunshot?" cried Gerda. "Will we get killed?"

"Quiet!" snapped Riley, frowning at Gerda until she ducked her head and closed her mouth.

"I didn't hear anything," said Sadie quietly. Apple sidestepped restlessly, and Sadie pulled her up short.

"Follow me, but keep quiet," said Riley, giving Gerda a warning look. He wanted to tell Sadie to wait right there for him, but he couldn't take a chance on anything happening to her and Gerda. It was safer to stay together.

A shiver ran down Sadie's spine as she followed Riley to the creek. Would they run into trouble like they had a few days ago? She didn't want to be shot at or kept a prisoner ever again. She wanted to go home where her family was waiting for them. Riley had said Momma and Caleb had gone to Vida to get papers so all of them would be Yorks legal-like. Sadie longed to go home, even if home was only a two-room sod house. To her surprise she felt more at home on the Circle Y than she'd ever felt back in Douglas County with the wood frame house, neighbors, and a school to attend. The closest school to them now was at Jake's Crossing, so Momma had said she'd teach them herself. But would they ever get home so Momma could? A cold knot tightened in Sadie's stomach.

Riley rode along a narrow creek, then stopped at the bend. He held a finger to his lips, then silently slipped off Bay in the shade of a small cottonwood.

Sadie's mouth turned bone-dry as she helped Gerda down, then dropped to the ground beside her. What had Riley heard? Sadie listened with everything in her, but she couldn't hear anything but the flow of the creek and a meadowlark singing from a piece of timothy grass.

"I don't hear a thing," said Gerda impatiently.

Riley gripped her arm and pushed his face down close to hers. "Do you want to get us killed?" he whispered gruffly.

Gerda whimpered and moved close to Sadie. She was a head taller than Sadie, and looked as old as Opal even though Gerda had said she was thirteen.

Sadie slipped her arm around Apple's head to keep her from nickering. Sadie glanced at Gerda. Maybe she should clamp her hand over Gerda's big mouth to keep her from making noise too.

Just then Sadie heard a rumble of men's voices and the clip-clop of horses' hooves.

Was danger just around the bend?

25

3
The Hanging

Riley dropped Bay's reins, and they dangled down to touch the ground. As long as the reins were down, Bay wouldn't move. Caleb had trained his horses that way. His stomach a tight knot, Riley inched his rifle from the boot and held it ready. He knew Pa's Navy Colt was tucked away safely in his bedroll, but it was no good to him without ammunition. "Stay behind me," he whispered. "And don't talk!" he ordered, looking right at Gerda.

Trembling, Sadie dropped Apple's reins and followed Riley. Gerda stuck as close to Sadie as a sandbur. Tension crackled in the air.

"What's going on?" whispered Gerda, plucking at Sadie's arm.

Sadie scowled at Gerda. "Shhh!"

"But what's happening?" she whispered, shiv-

27

ering even though the constant Nebraska wind was hot.

"I don't know," hissed Sadie. Couldn't Gerda see that she might be putting them in danger? "We'll know soon."

Gerda trembled. Before her family moved to the sandhills of Nebraska she'd never done anything more exciting than going sledding down a steep hill with trees at the bottom. By the gun in Riley's hand she knew there was more to be concerned about than running headlong into a tree.

Riley ducked behind a grassy knoll with grass up to his knees, and Sadie and Gerda followed. Carefully Riley peeked around the knoll. Two men stood in the shade of a small cottonwood facing Levi Cass. Levi had his hands tied behind his back, and he was bruised and bleeding. A few feet away a string of horses drank from the creek beside the men's saddled horses and Levi's mare Netty. Riley's neck muscles knotted. The men didn't look like buffalo hunters that captured people to use as slaves. They looked more like angry cowboys.

Sadie caught a glimpse of Levi, and her heart almost stopped. Why did the men have Levi tied up? He was as big as a full-grown man, but anyone could see he was still a boy. She wanted to leap up and demand they release Levi, but she stayed hidden in the tall grass. She glanced at Gerda beside her and willed her to keep her mouth shut. Nothing must happen to Levi Cass!

As Gerda looked at Levi Cass, a strange feeling rose up inside her. There was something about the way he stood before the men, his head high, his brown hair blowing in the wind and his brown eyes flashing, that tugged at her heart. He was in a bad spot, but he wasn't crying about it. She wanted to run to him and shield him from harm. She wanted to save him! This was a new feeling for Gerda, and she couldn't understand it at all.

The ropes around Levi's wrists cut into him deeply, and he forced back a cry of pain. He felt battered, worse than when he'd been bucked off a wild horse, but he would not let the two men know it! Warm wind dried the blood on his face and the sweat on his shirt. He stared at the men, whose names were Frayne and Rebel.

"You got any last words to say, boy?" asked Frayne, who was obviously in charge. He was tall and broad with a wide-brimmed gray hat with a snakeskin band.

Levi took a deep breath. "I told you I didn't steal your horses . . . I found them! That's the truth, and I won't say no different no matter what you do to me!"

"Don't spin no yarns now, boy!" snapped Rebel, a thin man with a drooping handlebar mustache. "You took them horses, and you'll get your neck stretched for it."

Sadie clamped her hand over her mouth to keep from crying aloud. She shot a frightened look at the tree branch above the men. They meant to hang Levi!

Riley's stomach rolled, and fear pricked his skin. It was up to him to set Levi free. But could he do it? He remembered that God was always with him, and silently he prayed for help.

Gerda couldn't understand what the man meant by stretching Levi's neck, but she could tell by the look of fear passing over Levi's face that it wasn't good news.

With a dark scowl, Rebel lifted a rope off his

saddle horn. "We got us a rope, a tree, and a horse thief. That means a party to me, Frayne."

Frayne pulled off his hat and slapped dust from it. "We gonna talk all day or are we gonna get down to the serious business of hangin' this thief? Get the boy's mare."

Sadie shivered. A grasshopper landed on her arm, and she bit back a gasp. A long-legged killdeer ran along the side of the creek.

Gerda bit her bottom lip. The men were actually planning to hang Levi Cass! She'd never seen anyone hung before except in a picture on a dime novel that Ma had forbade her to read. A picture of Levi dangling from the end of a rope with his tongue hanging out and his neck broke sent a wave of nausea over her. Oh, she couldn't let them hang Levi!

Before she had time to think about her actions, Gerda jumped up and ran around the knoll, her calico skirts flapping against her legs. Her sunbonnet bounced on her back between her shoulder blades as she covered the distance. She caught Levi's arm and faced the men, her skin sickly pale and her dark eyes wide with pleading. "Don't hurt him! Don't hang him!" The men gaped at her, and Levi stared at her as if he were seeing a ghost.

Riley looked helplessly on, his knuckles white as he gripped his rifle.

Sadie sank lower in the tall grass, anger rushing through her. How could Gerda be so stupid? Had she lived all her thirteen years without any brains?

"Where'd you come from, missy?" asked Frayne in surprise.

"From Michigan where people are civilized!" snapped Gerda with her chin high and her dark hair flowing down over her shoulders.

Rebel shot a look around. "You walk all the way from Michigan by your lonesome?" he asked, slapping the coiled rope against his leg as he took a step toward Gerda and Levi.

"I came with my family, but they're not with me right now." Gerda stepped behind Levi. "I'm going to untie his hands and let him go!"

"You'll do no such thing, missy! Get away from him," snapped Frayne. "You don't have no right to set him free. He stole our horses and he'll swing for it. That's the law of the land."

"He didn't steal them!" cried Gerda. She nudged Levi. "Did you?"

"No," he said, staring at her with open admiration.

Sadie saw the look, and jealousy ripped through her. She should've been the one to jump out and stop the men from hanging Levi, but she'd stayed back in the safety of the tall grass.

Riley steeled himself against taking the action he knew he'd have to take, but then he stood, his rifle cocked. "Levi is not a horse thief. Turn him loose . . . now!" His voice rang out with authority, and he sounded like Caleb York at his most commanding moment.

The men stared at Riley, then at Gerda, and back at Riley.

Sadie slowly stood, and the men turned their eyes on her. She trembled, but stood her ground.

"Did school just let out?" asked Rebel, scratching his head. "I never seen so many school kids smack in the middle of nowhere before."

"Kid, you point that rifle at me you better be ready to use it," said Frayne gruffly, his hand on the butt of his Colt.

"I don't want to use it," said Riley. Butterflies

31

fluttered in his stomach, but he looked calm and in control. "But I will if you make me."

"He means it," said Rebel softly. "Don't press him none."

Chills ran down Sadie's spine. She hated to think of Riley shooting anyone, but she could see by his face he'd shoot before he'd let them hang Levi.

"You kids go back where you belong before you get hurt," said Frayne gruffly. "We got a hangin' to see to."

"Do you know Caleb York?" asked Riley, keeping the rifle steady.

"Heard tell of him," said Frayne.

"I'm Riley York, and this is my sister Sadie. Caleb York is our daddy." Riley motioned to Levi. "And this is Levi Cass. His pa is a friend to Caleb York. His pa is Joshua Cass, the man who sees that law is upheld in these parts where there's no lawman. Joshua Cass's son wouldn't steal horses."

Frayne studied Riley's face, then finally said, "I reckon we best believe this boy."

With a string of swear words that burned Sadie's ears Rebel caught Frayne's arm. "Ain't I got no say?"

"Me and this rifle got the say for you," said Riley in a grim voice. "Let him go!"

The men shrugged. Netty nickered, and Apple answered.

"Sadie, get our horses," said Riley.

Sadie nodded, then ran around the knoll and led Bay and Apple to the creek. As they drank, she walked to the small tree nearby and leaned against it. She stared down at her overalls and suddenly felt ugly. She couldn't look at Levi without seeing

Gerda, and she didn't want to see the look on Gerda's face.

Gerda worked on the rope, breaking two fingernails, but she kept working until finally Levi was free.

He rubbed his wrists and smiled at her. She smiled back, and Sadie wanted to hit her. Levi and Gerda walked over to Riley side by side. Levi greeted Riley and Sadie, but quickly turned his attention back to Gerda. "Thanks," he whispered.

Gerda smiled up at him as if she were hopelessly in love.

Sadie knotted her fists, but didn't knock Gerda down like she wanted to.

"You better tell us your story from the beginning," said Frayne, pushing his hat back. "If you didn't steal our horses, who did?"

Levi picked up his hat from the ground where it had fallen when the men jumped him. He glanced at Riley and Sadie, then suddenly remembered they knew his terrible secret: his pa, Joshua Cass, was married to a Pawnee. Flushing, Levi forced back those thoughts and put his mind on what he was saying.

"You don't have to talk if you don't want to," said Gerda.

"He'll talk," snapped Frayne.

Riley lowered his rifle, but stood ready to use it if he had to.

Levi settled his hat in place, wincing at the pain when he touched a lump on his head. "I was out walkin' a few days ago, and I saw a small herd of horses grazing alone. I knew by their brands they weren't from around here. I figured I'd better corral them so Paw could see they got back where they belonged when he got home. I got Netty and a rope

33

and rode out after 'em. It took me a good while to catch all five of 'em. I strung 'em together and was leading them back when you jumped me."

Frayne scratched his head. "You say them horses were walking around by themselves? Then who was it stole 'em from us?"

"And where is he?" asked Rebel.

Sadie thought of the Indian, glanced at Riley, and knew she'd better not mention the warrior.

"I didn't see hide nor hair of anyone," said Levi. "Except that peddler, Cotton Twyll."

Sadie glanced up. Levi had no way of knowing what she and Riley knew—that the peddler was a thief and a liar. "Did he see you?"

"No. I stayed out of sight," said Levi. At that time he hadn't wanted to see or speak to anyone.

Riley took a step forward. "We ran into Cotton Twyll a few days ago. He had stolen my pa's Navy Colt and some other items. Could be he stole those horses and they got away from him."

"There was a peddler hangin' around the ranch a while back," said Frayne. "White hair . . . short and lean?"

"That's him," said Riley and Levi at the same time.

"If he did take 'em, I got a score to settle with him," said Rebel, twirling his mustache.

"We got our horses, so we best get back to the ranch and forget about settling a score," said Frayne. "We got work to catch up on."

Rebel hiked up his pants and nodded. "You're sure right about that." He looked at Levi and grinned. "No hard feelings, boy."

Levi hesitated, then shook his head.

"You should both be sent to jail!" cried Gerda, her eyes flashing. "What you did was wrong!"

Sadie tensed, and she saw that Riley did too. If the men wanted they could shoot all of them, take their horses, and ride away.

"We'll let that slide," said Frayne, eyeing Gerda coldly. "You don't know our ways."

"That's right," said Riley, wondering if he'd have time to lift his rifle and fire before Frayne or Rebel could draw.

"I would never hang anyone," said Gerda with a flip of her head.

"They let me go," said Levi softly to Gerda. "It's all over. Don't say another word."

Gerda saw the fear in Levi's eyes and decided she'd better keep quiet.

Sadie longed for Gerda to be back in Michigan where she belonged, but Sadie didn't speak or move. Finally the men walked to their horses, mounted, and rode away, leading the string of horses after them.

With a ragged sigh Sadie sank back against the tree and closed her eyes. Finally they could go home to hear all about being Yorks legal-like.

Suddenly a rifle cracked, and dirt scattered near Sadie's feet.

Cotton Twyll

Sadie screamed and leaped away even though she knew the bullet hadn't actually hit her. Riley stood several feet away with his rifle still aimed at a long rattlesnake wriggling inches from where Sadie had been standing. With a shiver she stared down at it. "I didn't hear it," she whispered.

"I want to go back to Michigan!" wailed Gerda, clinging to Levi's arm.

Riley walked to the twitching rattler and looked down at it. "I might not be able to shoot the wings off a fly like you, Sadie, but I got it before it got you."

Sadie brushed sweat off her face. "Thanks, Riley."

"Let's skin it and cut off its rattles," said Riley.

"Oh, don't touch it!" cried Gerda, hanging back as Levi walked to Riley's side.

"Good clean shot," said Levi, grinning at Riley. "Right behind the head."

Riley smiled, feeling proud as he handed the rifle to Sadie, then pulled out his knife and with Levi's help quickly cut off the rattles and skinned the snake.

Sadie wrinkled her nose at the strong snake odor. She glanced at Gerda, then grinned as Gerda turned away with one hand on her stomach and the other over her mouth. Sadie bit back a chuckle. Gerda was such a town girl! Levi wouldn't think she was so wonderful if he looked at her now. Sadie knew she should be nice to Gerda, but she said loud enough for Levi and Riley to hear, "Are you gonna throw up, Gerda?"

Gerda flushed to the roots of her dark hair. "No!"

Levi hurried to Gerda's side. "Are you all right?"

Gerda shot Sadie a withering look, but turned to Levi with a warm smile. "I guess all this excitement is too much for me. I'm not used to it."

Levi held her hand and patted it. "Maybe you should sit down a while."

"We have to get back," said Sadie sharply.

Riley tucked the rolled snakeskin in his bedroll, then reached for Bay's reins. "If it's all the same to you, Levi, me and Sadie will get on home. You take Gerda back to your place."

Sadie didn't like that at all. She hated to think of Gerda riding in the same saddle as Levi with her arms around him. Impatiently Sadie caught up Apple's reins and mounted. A little imp rose inside Sadie, and she turned to Levi. "Lost Sand Cherry will be glad you're safe, Levi."

Blushing, he ducked his head.

Sadie felt mean, but she said, "You shouldn't be ashamed that she's your mother."

Levi's eyes flashed. "She's not my mother! She's married to Pa, but she's not my ma!"

"I should think not!" cried Gerda, shaking her head. "I'd be afraid she'd scalp me if I lived with her."

Levi strode to Netty and leaped on her back. He knew Lost Sand Cherry would never scalp him, but he still hated having her married to his pa. Levi helped Gerda mount behind him. She slipped her arms around him, and his heart fluttered even more than when he saw Opal York.

Sadie's jaw tightened, and she looked quickly away from Gerda and Levi.

Riley reined up beside Levi. "Lost Sand Cherry was worried about you."

Levi shrugged. He didn't want to talk about her. "Thanks for helping me. I appreciate it."

"Anytime," said Riley with a grin. It felt good not to be angry at Levi the way he had been until just a day ago when the Lord had helped him get rid of his jealousy and anger. "Ride over to see us with Gerda and her folks if you can."

Sadie wanted to kick Riley.

Levi smiled and nodded. "I might do that."

"I hope you do," said Gerda, resting her head against Levi's strong back. He smelled sweaty and dusty, but she didn't care.

"Let's go, Riley," said Sadie impatiently. Apple moved restlessly, and Sadie nudged her ahead. It was past time to get home and let Momma know they were safe. Suddenly Sadie wondered why Caleb hadn't come after them. Maybe he had thought they could take care of themselves.

"Where're you going, Sadie?" called Riley.

"Home," she said over her shoulder.

He laughed. "Not that way you're not. Follow me." With a laugh he rode away from the creek and off into the vast prairie.

Sadie flushed and turned Apple to ride after Riley. Would she ever learn to read the hills the way Caleb did? She glanced at Gerda and Levi just in time to see them disappear around a small hill. Suddenly Sadie thought of the Indian warrior. Why hadn't she warned Levi about him even though Riley didn't want her to? "It's too late now," muttered Sadie.

She nudged Apple into a trot to catch up to Riley. A hawk soared across the sky. From the sun Sadie could see it was past high noon. Her stomach suddenly cramped with hunger. She'd have to wait until they got home to eat.

Excitement leaped inside her. Within two hours they'd be home with Caleb, Momma, Opal, Web, and Helen . . . and Tanner. She couldn't forget her dog! It seemed like it had been a month since she'd seen them all instead of only a few days.

Riley smiled back at Sadie, and they both slowed to a walk. "Won't Momma be happy to see family from Michigan!"

Sadie sighed and nodded. "I sure don't like Gerda for a cousin."

"She's headstrong all right."

"And a town girl!" To Sadie that was the worst insult she could give Gerda. "I hope they don't stay too long."

"Momma will want to hear all the Michigan news," said Riley. Down through the years he'd seen her write letters to her family. Because she was always short of paper, she'd only allow herself one page at a time. When it was filled, she'd turn it sideways and write over the top of what she'd already written. Riley hadn't been able to read it, but Momma had said her family could because they were used to it by now. Riley shifted in the saddle.

Someday when he had a ranch of his own he'd make enough cash money so Momma would have all the paper she needed, so she'd never have to write across her own words.

Sadie watched a flock of ducks fly overhead while Apple walked through the tall prairie grass waving in the warm wind. Just then something red in the grass caught Sadie's attention. "Look, Riley . . ." She pointed up ahead, then nudged Apple into a trot.

Riley narrowed his eyes as Bay ran to keep up with Sadie.

"It looks like a bolt of material like Cotton Twyll carried in his wagon." Sadie slipped from Apple's back and looked closer. "That's what it is, Riley." She gingerly picked it up and folded the unfurled length around the bolt, then held it under her arm as she mounted Apple. "Why would the old peddler just drop it here?"

"Maybe somebody else he cheated caught him and took it," said Riley, looking all around. He could only see the waving grass and the never-ending sky.

They rode for several minutes before Sadie sighted the peddler's wagon sitting at the side of a hill, hidden from their view until they were almost on it. She trembled. Something was wrong. The team of horses hitched to the wagon had their heads hanging down, seemingly too weary to nicker a greeting. And Cotton Twyll was nowhere in sight. Sadie gripped the reins tightly and waited for Riley to make the first move.

Riley slowly slipped from the saddle and walked cautiously around the wagon looking for the snow-white-haired peddler. "I don't see Cotton Twyll anywhere," he finally said.

"The team looks ready to drop. I'll water them."
Sadie lifted the water bucket from under the wagon
and filled it from the barrel at the side of the wagon,
then watered the horses. She could tell they were
thirsty. Maybe the Indian had killed and scalped
Cotton Twyll. Sadie shivered and shot a look
around. Or maybe Frayne and Rebel had run across
him, learned he had rustled their horses, and hung
him. There were too many holes in her story to
believe it, and she impatiently turned to Riley.

"Where could the peddler be?"

"Out there somewhere. It looks like the horses
ran hard before they finally stopped here. That bolt
of cloth probably bounced right out of the wagon."

Sadie studied the wagon carefully. The last
time she'd seen it, shovels, brooms, sickles, and
such hung down the outside of the covered wagon.
A couple of shovels and a sickle still hung on it. The
red and gold seat was covered with dust. In back
the tailgate was down and the flaps loose. Was the
wonderful wide-brimmed hat that she'd liked so
much still there? Oh, how she wanted that hat!
She'd tried it on and had admired herself in the
looking glass. She was far from beautiful like Opal,
but she had been more than passable in that hat.

She peered inside and gasped in alarm. The
goods were in shambles, and Cotton Twyll lay
among the shambles, an angry bruise on the side
of his face, his once snow-white hair caked with
dried blood. Flies buzzed around Cotton's head
and landed on his closed eyes. Sadie's stomach
rolled, and for a minute she thought she'd throw
up. Slowly she turned. "Riley, come here," she said
in a strangled voice.

He ran to her side, ready for anything. The
sight sickened him. From the way the flies buzzed
around Cotton Riley, he was sure he was dead.

Slowly Riley climbed inside and felt for a pulse. The smell turned his stomach. He found a weak pulse and glanced back at Sadie. "He's alive . . . barely."

Cotton moaned and opened his eyes. "Help me," he muttered.

"We will," said Riley. Cotton had stolen Pa's Navy Colt, but Riley knew he couldn't let that keep him from helping the man. It had taken a fight to get the Navy Colt back, but now it was tucked safely away in Riley's bedroll.

Sadie wanted to tell Cotton he was getting just what he deserved, but she didn't. She spotted the hat she wanted so badly, but she didn't touch it. She could've taken it and worn it and called it her own, but that would be stealing. And she knew stealing was wrong.

"What happened to you?" asked Riley, looking carefully at the wounds.

"Horses spooked . . . Ran away." Cotton gasped and weakly lifted a hand, then let it fall. "Hit my head."

"Get water for him, Sadie," said Riley.

Sadie quickly filled a dipper with lukewarm water from the barrel and handed it to Riley.

He carefully lifted Cotton and helped him drink. Riley saw the edge of a plow where Cotton's head had struck. It was a wonder the peddler was still alive.

Cotton moaned, and his head rolled.

"What'll we do?" asked Sadie in alarm.

"The Cass ranch is closer than ours, so we'll take him there. I'll drive, and you ride alongside on Apple." Riley settled the unconscious Cotton as comfortably as he could, tied Bay's reins to the back of the wagon, then ran around and climbed up on the high red and gold seat. He gathered the reins in his hands and slapped them on the team.

Sadie groaned at the thought of seeing Gerda

so soon, but she rode beside the wagon, alert for any sign of danger. The wagon rattled so loud she couldn't make Riley hear her unless she shouted, so she kept her questions and thoughts to herself.

She touched her bonnet, then glanced at the back of the wagon. "I want that hat," she muttered. Maybe with that hat Levi would think she was beautiful. He might tell Gerda to keep her hands off him because he liked Sadie Rose York. Oh, but she wanted that hat! Then she hung her head in shame. It was a sin to covet.

"Forgive me, Jesus. I will be thankful for what I have. Honest I will!" She touched her limp, faded bonnet. It did keep the hot sun off her head. It did shade her face. It was better than no hat at all! "Someday, though, I want a handsome wide-brimmed hat all my own."

She looked off across the prairie with the peddler's wagon creaking beside her. Suddenly all thoughts of the hat and how wonderful she'd look in it faded from her thoughts. Up ahead was the valley where the Cass ranch lay. Up ahead she'd have to face Levi and Gerda together.

A grasshopper landed on Sadie's faded overalls, and she slapped it away before it could spit tobacco juice on her.

After their ride together would Levi be hopelessly in love with Gerda?

Sadie groaned.

"I hate Gerda even if she is my cousin," muttered Sadie. The terrible words hung in the air and seemed to drift down over her and cover her with a heavy black cloud.

5

Geronimo

Sadie thankfully ate the last bite of stew Lost Sand Cherry had given her, finished her last morsel of bread, and drank her milk. She'd almost turned the meal down, but Riley had agreed to eat, and Sadie had finally given in. Now she was thankful. She'd been hungrier than she'd thought.

She peeked across the room at Levi and Gerda whispering in the corner. Sadie frowned down at her empty plate. Levi hardly noticed she was there.

Lost Sand Cherry was still in the bedroom doctoring Cotton Twyll.

Just then the door opened, and Mart Tasker walked in with Essie and the baby right behind him. Mart was younger than Caleb, but as tall and muscular. His blond hair hung in tangles to his shoulders, and dark smudges circled his blue eyes.

Sadie and Riley had met him outdoors when they'd first arrived.

"Sadie . . ." Mart clamped a large hand on her shoulder and smiled down at her. "Riley . . ." He shook hands with Riley again. "Any family of Essie's is a family to me." He straddled a chair backwards and rested his arms across the back of it while Essie took the baby to the rocking chair. "It seems you two ran into some trouble. Gerda's not quit talking about it since she and Levi got back."

Sadie looked helplessly at Riley. She didn't know if she was supposed to speak or be quiet. Mart liked to talk—that she'd learned when they first arrived with Cotton.

"We were ready to head out for your place when you brought that peddler man here." Mart brushed his hair back and shook his head. "I got the grave started and will finish it if it comes to that . . . Unless Levi over there wants the job."

Levi glanced up at the sound of his name, but turned right back to whispering with Gerda.

Sadie locked her hands together in her lap. Levi had never talked this much, even to Opal.

"I can't imagine there being no law around here," said Mart, shaking his head. "What would you do if Geronimo raided you?"

Sadie had heard of the Indian and his attacks, but she hadn't thought about him coming to Nebraska. Suddenly the hair on the back of her neck stood on end. Was the warrior she'd seen Geronimo, the most feared Indian of the day? "I saw a warrior," she blurted out.

Riley jabbed her arm. "Stop it! This is not the time to tease."

He scowled so fiercely at Sadie that she didn't dare say another word about the Indian.

"Sadie likes to tease, eh?" Mart chuckled. "It don't seem like wild Indians would be a thing to tease about around here."

Sadie sank lower in her chair and hung her head. Why couldn't she make Riley believe her?

"You're probably wondering what made me bring my family way out here to Nebraska," said Mart.

Sadie hadn't wondered that at all, but she didn't say so. She noticed Riley didn't either.

"I figured folks are coming here right and left. Folks need houses. I came to build houses. That's what I do . . . Build houses." He sighed heavily. "Never knew there weren't trees around here, though. I guess that's why the lumbermen of Michigan are shipping wood here. The man in Jake's Crossing said folks build sod houses mostly since they can't afford to build frame houses. Now that puts me in a pickle, so to speak."

Lost Sand Cherry walked through with a pan of bloody water, and Sadie jumped up to see if she could help her.

"Stay with him while I am out," said Lost Sand Cherry without a smile. "He lost a lot of blood."

Sadie reluctantly walked into the bedroom. It smelled closed in. She stood over the bed where Cotton lay. His skin was as white as his hair, and he looked very frail.

Cotton opened his eyes. "Indian," he muttered.

"It's Joshua Cass's wife, Lost Sand Cherry," said Sadie softly.

"Indian brave," he mumbled.

Sadie's heart almost leaped from her chest. "What about him?"

"Spooked horses . . . War paint."

47

"Riley says all the Indian braves are on reservations," said Sadie, barely able to speak.

"Warrior." Cotton tried to raise his head, but was too weak. "Big! War paint!"

Sadie bent low over Cotton. "Did you see him?"

"War paint! Kill us all!"

"I saw him too!" said Sadie hoarsely. Muttering, Cotton thrashed around.

Sadie held him down, fearing he'd die before her eyes. "Please lie still."

"Don't . . . want . . . to . . . die."

Sadie bit her lip. What should she do? "Do you want me to pray for you?" asked Sadie hesitantly.

"Pray," whispered Cotton. He rambled on and on while Sadie quietly prayed beside his bed.

Lost Sand Cherry slipped in silently and stood at the foot of the bed. "His mind is gone," she said. "Soon he will go to meet his Maker."

Sadie gripped her hands together in front of her.

Lost Sand Cherry walked to the head of the bed and leaned down to Cotton. "Are you ready to meet God, Cotton Twyll?"

He grew quiet and opened his eyes, focusing them on Lost Sand Cherry. "No," he muttered, plucking at the sheet. "Help me."

Tears burned the backs of Sadie's eyes.

"Ask Jesus to forgive your sins and cleanse your heart," said Lost Sand Cherry in a gentle voice.

"Help me," whispered Cotton weakly.

Lost Sand Cherry leaned her head closer to Cotton's. "Jesus, forgive me. I give myself to You."

Cotton weakly repeated, "Jesus, forgive me. I give myself to You." He grew quiet.

Sadie felt peace fill the room. As she stood

there, Cotton closed his eyes and died. She knew the real Cotton had gone to be with the Lord, and only his body had stayed behind to be buried. She thought it would frighten her to see death, but it didn't. Cotton was probably talking with Jesus right now.

Lost Sand Cherry covered Cotton's face, then walked with Sadie to the other room. "He is gone," she said. "He made his peace with God first."

"I got his box built and his grave started," said Mart. They'd already learned he had no family and no friends. They had agreed to bury him near Levi's mother's grave.

Sadie stepped close to Riley.

"I won't stay in the same house with a dead man!" cried Gerda, running for the door.

Levi started after her, but Riley stopped him. "You'll have to help me carry him out to the grave," Riley said.

Levi trembled. He'd watched his pa carry his ma to the grave he'd dug, lay her in a rough box, and slide her down in the hole, then drop dirt over her. He had never forgotten it. He couldn't watch another burying! He didn't want to hear the dirt hit the box. He didn't want to see death again! "I can't do it," he said hoarsely.

"I will help," said Lost Sand Cherry, touching Levi's arm.

Levi jerked away from her. "Nobody asked for your help!"

Riley frowned. "I can't carry him alone."

"I'll do it," said Levi gruffly.

Several minutes later Cotton Twyll was buried. The sun was low in the west. The silence stretched on and was finally broken with the baby's loud cry.

"We have to go," Riley said as he settled his hat in place.

"What about the old man's things?" asked Mart.

"Joshua Cass will decide what to do with them," said Riley. He'd unhitched the peddler's horses and put them in the corral just after they'd arrived. The wagon stood outside the sod barn.

Sadie didn't want to, but she thought about the hat in the back of Cotton's wagon as they all walked toward the corral fence to get Bay and Apple. No one would care if she took the hat. Abruptly she pushed the bad thought away. It wasn't hers to take just because Cotton Twyll was dead.

"I wonder if we'll ever know what happened to cause the old peddler's death," said Mart as they passed the wagon.

Sadie's heart raced, and she darted a look at Riley. She stopped beside Apple. "I know what caused it," she said in a voice that seemed too loud.

Everyone turned to stare at her. Riley frowned, having an idea of what to expect but not being sure.

"What?" asked Mart.

"An Indian warrior spooked his team," said Sadie weakly.

"Sadie!" Riley gripped her arm. He wanted to shake her, but he didn't.

Sadie pulled away from Riley and lifted her chin high. "Cotton saw the Indian . . . And so did I! I saw an Indian warrior this morning! He was big and had on war paint!"

Mart whistled. Gerda screamed, but nobody paid attention to her.

"I give up," said Riley grimly.

Lost Sand Cherry took Sadie's hand and held

it firmly. "There are no Indians with war paint in these parts, Sadie."

"But I saw him!"

"Tell us what he looked like," said Mart. "I want to know what's out there! You think I want my whole family scalped?"

Gerda screamed again and clung to Levi's arm.

Levi was still thinking about his mother and death and dropping dirt on the grave. Sadie's words hadn't gotten past his misery.

"Sadie, don't say another word," said Riley with a stern look.

"Let her talk," said Mart. "I want to hear about the Indian she saw."

Sadie took a deep breath, then told about the warrior.

Lost Sand Cherry sagged against the fence. "You say he had hair that looked like a horn?"

"Yes."

Riley looked in surprise at Lost Sand Cherry. Why was she suddenly alarmed? She never let it show when something upset her.

"What does that mean to you, Cherry?" asked Mart.

"Pawnee warrior," whispered Lost Sand Cherry. "But that is not possible!"

"I saw him!" cried Sadie. "He looked right at me!"

"I'm not staying out here in the open where I'll get scalped!" Gerda tugged on Levi's arm, but when he wouldn't move, she ran to the house and slammed the door after her.

"Is it Geronimo?" asked Sadie.

"He's a Chiricahua," said Riley, "fighting in Arizona. Daddy was talking about him just last week. He wouldn't come here."

51

"Pawnee braves put their hair up like horn," said Lost Sand Cherry, once again in control of herself. "That is why some have called them the Horn People."

"We must be very careful," said Mart, gazing all around the valley and off into the prairie. He turned back to Riley. "We'll travel together to York's place. How long will it take us to get there?"

"About two hours," said Riley.

"Levi and Cherry, you must go with us," said Mart. It seemed strange for anyone to shorten Lost Sand Cherry's name, but Mart didn't give it a thought.

"We will wait here for Joshua," said Lost Sand Cherry in great dignity.

"I'll go with you," said Levi quickly. He didn't want to stay here with his memories.

"But you can't leave Lost Sand Cherry alone," said Sadie. Sometimes she wondered how she could like Levi in the special way that made her heart beat faster.

After thinking through all that Sadie had said, Riley shook his head. "Sadie, why did you say anything about seeing an Indian warrior? You know you didn't see any such thing."

"Use your head, boy! How else would she know what a Pawnee warrior looks like?" asked Mart.

"She made it up," said Riley.

Sadie squared her shoulders and lifted her chin. "I did not!"

A muscle jerked in Riley's jaw. "Sadie Rose York, you're scaring everybody for no reason. Now tell them it's a joke. I mean it, Sadie."

Tears welled up in Sadie's eyes. Riley should know she wouldn't carry a joke this far. She wanted to beg him to believe her, but she knew she'd burst into tears if she said anything. She turned away and tightened Apple's cinch strap.

Anger and embarrassment burned inside Riley. If Caleb were here, he would get Sadie to take back her wild story.

Mart touched Riley's arm. "Don't be so hard on her. She looks like she's telling the truth. I, for one, believe her."

Riley reached for Bay's cinch strap. "I don't!"

Sadie heard him, and a tear spilled down her cheek. She flicked it away and blinked hard to hold the others back. She would not cry!

6
Gerda

Stroking Apple's sleek neck, Sadie looked longingly across the prairie. She wanted to race like the wind back to the Circle Y instead of staying with the Taskers' slow-moving covered wagon. She wanted to race with Tanner and know that he was her dog even though she had to share him with the family. She even wanted to pick up dried cow chips with Helen and Web, then have Momma remind them not to pick up wet ones. But most of all she wanted to tell Caleb about the Indian she'd seen and have him believe her and do something about it.

She glanced at Riley leading the way on Bay. She knew he was still upset with her. She didn't look at Levi and Gerda on Netty to the left of the wagon. Levi was acting so dumb! How could he think Gerda was so wonderful just because she'd helped save his life? Riley had been the one who'd actually saved him from Frayne and Rebel. Levi sure hadn't invited Riley to ride double with him!

Just then Gerda shouted to her pa, and Levi turned Netty in close to the swaying wagon.

"Pa, I left my kaleidoscope at Levi's house!" cried Gerda. "I have to have it. Can we turn around and go back for it?"

"Sorry, Gerda," said Mart, shaking his head. "We can't."

"You have to!" cried Gerda. "You have to turn around and go back right now!"

Sadie's face burned with shame for Gerda. How could anyone be so naughty? If Sadie acted that way Momma would spank her, even at the great age of twelve. Didn't Gerda's folks ever spank her?

"I told you to leave it in the wagon, Gerda," said Essie from where she sat beside Mart.

"I wanted to show it to Levi," said Gerda with a pout. "Levi, can you ride back and get it for me? You can catch up to us if you ride fast, can't you?"

Sadie gasped. Gerda knew about the Indian warrior, yet she asked Levi to go back for her toy! This was beyond anything Sadie had heard yet! A toy, even such an unusual one that showed marvelous colors and designs like she'd never even imagined, wasn't worth a life!

"I left it at the well when I got a drink before we left," said Gerda. "Please, Levi . . . please, please, get it for me."

"I'll go back," said Levi reluctantly. He wasn't concerned about danger, but he also didn't want to see the new grave or talk with Lost Sand Cherry. "It shouldn't take me too long."

Trembling, Sadie raced Apple around and

reined in close to Levi. "You can't go alone! You heard what I said about the Indian!"

Levi shrugged. "I can take care of myself." He figured Riley was right and that Sadie was playing a joke that she couldn't admit to without shaming herself.

Gerda scowled at Sadie. "You don't want him to go back for it because you're jealous. I have a kaleidoscope and you don't!"

Sadie's neck and face burned with embarrassment. Could the others believe such a thing of her? She had wanted to look at the colors and designs longer than her fair turn while Mart hooked up the team, but she was not jealous. She stared down at Apple's mane, unwilling to see what the others were thinking or feeling.

"Levi will get my kaleidoscope no matter what you say, Sadie York!" said Gerda. "Won't you, Levi?"

"I said I would," he said.

Riley glanced around, then rode back to see what was going on. The wagon had slowed to a crawl, and Sadie looked very upset. Was she telling them more tall tales? "What's going on?" he asked, looking right at Sadie.

She gripped the reins more tightly, but didn't answer.

Gerda said, "Riley, Levi says he'll ride back to his place and get my kaleidoscope and bring it to me, but Sadie is trying to stop him. Tell her to keep her thoughts to herself."

Riley looked up at Mart. "Can't Levi bring the toy to Gerda another time? We want to get to the Circle Y before dark."

Gerda glared at Riley. "Don't you dare make me wait! I want my kaleidoscope now! I won't wait another day for it!"

Mart sighed heavily. "Riley, we'll keep going while Levi rides back for the thing. It's Gerda's pride and joy, and she doesn't want to be without it." Mart looked at Levi. "Are you sure you're not worried about that Indian Sadie saw?"

"I'm not," said Levi. "I can take care of myself."

Sadie bit her tongue to keep back the rush of angry words inside her.

"Gerda, you climb into the wagon and let Levi head back," said Mart.

"I'll ride with Sadie," said Gerda.

Sadie's head shot up. "No!"

Riley turned to Sadie in surprise, then decided to let her handle the matter herself. He wouldn't want Gerda riding with him either.

Mart sighed again. "Sadie, let her ride with you, will you . . . please? It'll help keep peace."

Sadie's stomach knotted. Momma had told her over and over to obey adults. How she wanted to tell Mart Tasker that she wouldn't let Gerda ride with her no matter how much she pouted and screamed. But she didn't. She nodded slightly.

"Thank you, Sadie," said Essie.

Levi rode close to Apple, held Gerda's arm, and eased her over behind Sadie. "I'll be back soon," he said.

"Thanks, Levi," said Gerda sweetly.

He smiled at Gerda, looked briefly at Sadie, and galloped back toward his home. Netty's tail flew out like a long black flag, and Levi's shirt billowed out from his back.

"Let's get a move on," said Mart, slapping the reins against his team. The harness rattled, and the wagon creaked as it rolled faster.

Gerda clung to Sadie's overall straps. "Don't

make me fall off or you'll be sorry," she said close to Sadie's ear.

Sadie clamped her mouth closed and nudged Apple to catch up to Bay. The sun was so slow in the west that Sadie knew it wouldn't be long before darkness would come. Would Levi make it back before dark? If so, he'd have to do some hard riding.

"We can at least talk, can't we?" asked Gerda.

Sadie hesitated. She was angry and tired, and her whole body felt gritty with sand. Her braids were coming loose, and her hair hung in tangles below her bonnet. She wanted to snap at Gerda, but she knew that would be wrong. "I guess so," she finally said.

"Is it true about that Indian warrior?" asked Gerda sharply.

"Yes."

"I don't believe you!"

"Then why did you ask?"

"I don't want Levi to get scalped."

"Neither do I!"

"You like him a lot, don't you?" asked Gerda with a jealous tinge to her voice.

Sadie would not let Gerda know just how much she did like Levi Cass. "I like him," she said with a shrug. "But he likes Opal better."

"Your sister?"

"Yes. She's fifteen and pretty. She says she might marry Levi when they're old enough." Sadie didn't tell Gerda that Opal wanted to get married when she turned sixteen and looked at all fine young men with that in mind.

"Well, she can't marry him. I intend to."

Sadie rolled her eyes. "You're only thirteen."

"I'm almost seventeen! But Ma makes me say

I'm thirteen so nobody will know how young she was when she had me."

Sadie turned her head, but couldn't see Gerda's face to know if she was lying. "I never heard of such a thing before."

"I always get my own way with Ma and Pa because they know I'll tell the secret if I don't."

"You just told me the secret."

Gerda laughed softly. "But if you tell anyone, I'll just say you're lying or that I was only teasing and you took it for truth."

Sadie couldn't believe her ears. She'd never met such a bad girl in all her life. "Aren't you afraid for Levi with that warrior out in the prairie?"

"Levi said he can take care of himself. And he looks like he can."

"But he didn't believe me, so he won't be on the lookout."

Gerda trembled. "You mean you were telling the truth?"

Sadie's jaw tightened. "Yes. I said I was."

Gerda whimpered and pressed her forehead against Sadie's back. "I don't want anything to happen to Levi. I only want my kaleidoscope." She lifted her head. "You could send Riley after Levi."

Sadie shook her head. "He wouldn't go."

"Pa will make him."

"He can't." Sadie was torn between wanting Riley to make sure Levi was safe and keeping Gerda from having her own way. "Riley's leading us all home."

Gerda was quiet a long time. Wind tangled her mass of dark hair. "You could lead us."

"I don't know the way." Sadie could read the hills on the Circle Y and across to the Hepfords, but she didn't know the way to Jake's Crossing or the

Cass ranch. She didn't even know the way to Jewel Comstock's place where her best friend Mary lived. "There aren't roads . . . just wagon tracks across the prairie, and usually you can't see them."

"No roads? That's crazy!"

"That's the way it is out in the sandhills. Caleb says it won't always be that way, but it is now."

Gerda looked back where Levi had gone, but there was no sign of him. "What if Levi gets lost?"

"He won't. He was born and raised here. And he can track."

"What does that mean?"

"He can look at the ground, find a horse or wagon track, and follow it until he finds it." Sadie watched a cottontail hop from one clump of grass to another. A herd of antelope raced across the crest of a hill, then disappeared in the distance.

"Folks here sure are different from Michigan people."

Sadie shifted in the saddle. She knew not all Michigan people were like Gerda. "Momma says there are trees everywhere in Michigan."

"There are."

"And rocks . . . Big rocks."

"Aren't there rocks here?"

"Little ones." Sadie looked around. Suddenly she knew where she was. "We're on the Circle Y," she said excitedly.

"Where's the house?"

"It's still a ways off." The huge red sun slipped behind a hill, but Sadie knew they'd be home before the sky turned dark and the stars came out. "Up ahead of Riley as far as you can see is Caleb York's ranch."

"He's not your real pa, is he?"

"He's our daddy! And he got a paper making us

his legal children." Sadie flushed with pride. "He never had a family before us. He said a rancher in Texas found him crying under a cactus when he was just a baby, took him home with him, and named him York after the place where *he* was born. He didn't have a first name until we gave him one . . . Caleb. We named him that because in the Bible Caleb was one of the spies who gave a good report to Moses. Our Caleb always has good things to say. He's a fine man. And he loves us all."

"I think I'll like him," said Gerda with longing in her voice.

Sadie knew Caleb would think Gerda was a spoiled, headstrong girl, but she didn't say that.

"Where is Levi?" asked Gerda, sounding worried. "He said he'd be back before we got to your place."

"He said he'd try," said Sadie.

A few minutes later Sadie saw the barn and the two houses in the distance. One lone tree, Momma's tree, stood in front of the bigger house. Caleb had transplanted it from Cottonwood Creek as a surprise for Momma. Tears stung Sadie's eyes, and her heart leaped. Finally she was home.

"Where's your house?" asked Gerda.

"We live in the one with the tree."

"But that's not a house!"

"It's a sod house."

"Sod house? You mean you live in a house made from dirt from the ground?"

Sadie tried to explain about cutting chunks of sod from the prairie and stacking them up like giant bricks, but Gerda interrupted her to ask about Levi again.

Just then Riley turned Bay and rode back to Sadie. "I figured Levi would be back before this."

Sadie's stomach cramped. "Me too."

Riley steadied Bay. "Maybe he decided to wait until morning."

"I hope he did," said Gerda in a low, tight voice.

Riley looked intently at Sadie. "Don't you tell Momma and the kids that crazy story about the Indian."

Sadie looked him right in the eye. "Riley, I have to tell Daddy. He'll want to find the Indian and keep him from killin' us all."

Suddenly Riley knew that Sadie had told the truth. He could see it in her face and hear it in her voice. Fear trickled over him.

And Sadie saw that Riley finally believed her. She wanted to laugh right out loud for gladness, but she couldn't. "I hope Levi's safe," she whispered.

7

Home!

Sadie left Gerda at the wagon with her parents, then galloped across the prairie beside Riley to greet the family in privacy. Pounding hooves rang in Sadie's ears. Wind tore off her bonnet and loosened the rest of her brown hair from its braids, whipping it into wild tangles around her thin shoulders. Her heart almost leaped out of her shirt at the sight of Momma waiting for her beside her tree. Momma looked so sturdy and calm. She wore her blue gingham dress that Sadie had helped sew.

"Sadie! Riley!" shouted Opal, Web, and Helen, waving excitedly as they ran toward the racing horses.

At the well Sadie sprang from the saddle and landed on the run. She reached Momma before Riley and flung her arms around her. "Oh,

Momma," said Sadie with tears welling up in her brown eyes that were so much like Momma's.

"Sadie, Sadie . . ." Momma gathered Sadie close to her plump body and held her tight. "Thank God you're home again and you're safe."

Sadie wanted to stay in Momma's arms, but she let her go so Riley could hug her. He towered over Momma, but he leaned down so she could hug him. Tears burned his eyes. "Momma, I'm glad to be back," he whispered. "We got a lot to tell."

"I want to hear it all," said Momma. "But we must see to our company first." Company always came first with Momma. She saw that guests were fed even if there wasn't much food left in the house. Momma liked it to be said that she set a good table and had good conversation.

"Where's Daddy?" asked Riley.

"Out hunting for you two," said Momma, dabbing tears from her eyes with her small white handkerchief.

Sadie gasped and shot a look at Riley. Would Caleb run across the warrior?

"We were scared for you," said Opal, blinking back tears.

"Real scared," said Helen, plucking at Sadie's arm.

Sadie hugged Helen, Web, and Opal while they all talked at once. She patted Tanner's head, then hugged everyone all over again. "It's good to be home," she said again.

"And who did you bring?" asked Momma, watching the wagon rolling toward them. The sun had set in the west, but it was still light out.

"You'll be surprised," said Riley as he clamped his hat back on his head. Essie had said she wanted to be the one to tell about being cousins, just to see the surprise on their faces. "Momma, they're from Michigan."

"Michigan!" cried Helen, bobbing around until her baby-fine white hair came loose from the braids. Each time someone had ridden into the yard Momma's first question was always, "Are you from Michigan?" Helen had waited all her eight years for someone from Michigan to visit.

Riley turned to nine-year-old Web. "See to Bay and Apple . . . And take the rattlesnake skin out of my bedroll and hang it over the fence until we can stretch it."

"How'd you kill it?" asked Web excitedly. He wanted every gory detail, but Riley said he'd tell him later.

Mart stopped the wagon and dropped to the ground in a puff of dust, then reached up for Essie and the sleeping baby. He turned back for Gerda, but she jumped down by herself, then smoothed down her dress and adjusted her bonnet.

"Momma, this is Mart and Essie Tasker with their baby Joey and their daughter Gerda," said Riley.

"So you're Bess Keller," said Essie.

Momma gasped, and the kids grew quiet around her. Sadie watched Momma's face expectantly.

"I was a Keller, but now I'm a York," said Momma. "Do you know my family?"

Mart chuckled.

"Tell her, Ma," said Gerda impatiently.

Essie's brown eyes twinkled. "Nathan Keller is my papa."

"Uncle Nate? . . . Your papa? . . . He's my papa's brother!"

Essie giggled and nodded. "We're cousins!"

Tears filled Momma's eyes, something that happened so seldom that Sadie felt tears sting her own eyes. Momma was not one to cry.

Momma hugged Essie, baby and all. "Cousins! Oh, I want to hear all the news! When did you leave Michigan? Did you see my family? How are they?" Momma pulled Essie toward the sod house as she shot question after question at her.

Helen ran after them. "I'll hold the baby while you talk." She didn't want to miss a word.

Riley introduced Mart and Gerda to the others. Mart talked to Riley and Web as they led the team to the barn to unhitch them.

Gerda studied Opal. "Sadie said you were pretty . . . And you are!" She sounded angry.

Opal flushed. Her nutmeg-brown hair was neatly braided, and her calico dress was clean and fresh-looking. The minute Web had spotted someone coming she'd changed clothes, rebraided her hair, and put on her shoes. She hated for anyone to see her barefoot and mussed. Opal smiled and said, "Could I get you a drink of water or something to eat?"

Gerda frowned and looked around. "It's getting dark! I'm too concerned about Levi to think about anything else!"

Opal turned to Sadie with a shocked look. "What about Levi?"

"He was supposed to be here by now," Sadie said simply. It would take too long to go into detail, and she had to speak with Riley.

"Would he come even though it's almost dark?" asked Gerda, sounding genuinely worried.

"I don't think so," said Sadie.

"You're scaring me," whispered Opal.

Fire shooting from her dark eyes, Gerda

68

turned on Opal. They were both the same height and build and looked alike, except Gerda's nose was bigger and her eyes were brown instead of blue. "You keep away from Levi! He's mine!"

With a gasp Opal fell back a step.

Sadie wanted to knock Gerda down a notch, but she said instead, "Let's go see if Riley thinks Levi will come yet tonight."

Flipping her flowing hair over her shoulder, Gerda ran off without waiting for Sadie.

"What is wrong with her?" whispered Opal, staring after Gerda.

"She's spoiled rotten," whispered Sadie. "We'll talk later. Let's go find Riley." She wanted to remind him Caleb was perhaps somewhere out there with the Indian.

When they reached Riley Gerda was saying, "What about Levi? Why isn't he here yet?"

"Maybe Joshua got back and told him to wait 'til morning . . . Or maybe Lost Sand Cherry did."

"Or maybe the warrior got him!" cried Gerda.

"What warrior?" asked Web and Opal at the same time.

"Never mind," said Riley.

"Some Indian is out there ready to scalp every-body!" snapped Gerda.

Opal leaned weakly against the Taskers' wagon while Web shot question after question at Riley.

Sadie glared at Gerda. They had agreed that only Caleb should be told about the Indian, then he could tell the others if he saw fit. "Why didn't you keep quiet about the Indian? You promised!"

Gerda stamped her foot, and dust puffed onto her black shoe. "I can do what I want! You can't scold me, Sadie!"

Riley gripped Gerda's arms and pushed his face down close to hers. "You stop that right now! It's your fault Levi is not here with us."

Gerda burst into tears and sagged against Riley, but he pushed her away. "I don't want Levi scalped!"

"Scalped?" whispered Opal, her blue eyes wide.

"Scalped?" cried Web excitedly. He'd always wanted to live during the time of the Indian wars, even though Momma had told him it was wrong to take another life.

Sadie shivered and looked out into the sudden darkness. Stars twinkled in the never-ending sky.

"I'm sure Levi will be here in the morning," said Riley.

"I hope so," said Gerda with a catch in her voice.

Sadie reached for Opal's hand and squeezed it reassuringly. "He'll be here," she said with more confidence than she felt.

The next morning Sadie finished milking Bossie and walked out of the sod barn with Tanner at her side. Today she wore her calico dress. It felt good to wear it instead of Riley's overalls and shirt. She watched the sky turn red. It was almost too early for the birds to be up, but still she scanned the prairie for Levi. She saw antelope and coyotes, but she didn't see Levi on Netty.

Slowly she carried the milk to the house and handed it to Opal to strain. Momma was at the stove frying pancakes for everyone. They'd all stayed up late into the night talking with the Taskers. Momma had wanted to hear all the news of the past eighteen years since she'd left Michigan.

Home!

Opal strained the milk and handed the pail back to Sadie. "Levi?" she mouthed.

"Not yet," whispered Sadie.

Opal looked ready to cry.

Sadie walked outdoors to rinse the empty milk pail at the well. She glanced toward the wagon where the Taskers had slept. She saw a movement, and then Gerda poked her head out the back of the wagon. She spotted Sadie, and a guilty looked crossed her face.

Sadie frowned. Now what was Gerda up to?

Gerda dropped to the ground, still in her night-dress and cap. Her feet were bare. She ran to Sadie and whispered, "Did Levi come yet?"

"No."

Gerda held out her hand. A long, round tube lay in it.

"Your kaleidoscope!" said Sadie in surprise.

Gerda ducked her head and flushed to the roots of her dark hair. "I found it last night, but I didn't say anything."

"You *found* it?"

"In my case. I forgot that I'd put it away. I really did think I'd left it on the well, but after I saw it last night I remembered running to the well to get it. But then Pa was talking crazy about the Indian and what we'd do if he jumped us and I forgot about putting the kaleidoscope in my case."

"So Levi went back for no reason!" Sadie burned with anger, and she clenched her fists at her sides. "He could be dead for all we know!"

Gerda burst into tears. "I know . . . I could hardly sleep thinking about him. Let's ride to his place and see if he's all right."

"I'd get lost by myself, and Riley is too busy to go with us."

71

"But we can't just do nothing!"

Sadie knew Riley had ridden off at the crack of dawn to check the windmill, the cattle and horses, and the fence. He wouldn't be back until late in the morning. And if he ran into trouble of any kind, he'd be back even later. Sadie sighed heavily. "You just better pray Levi comes riding in soon."

Gerda trembled and nodded.

By late morning Sadie was so frightened for Levi that she saddled Apple so she could head for the Cass ranch as soon as Riley came. When Riley did return he was dusty and hungry and tired, but he agreed they'd have to check on Levi. He took Momma aside and told her his plans.

After dinner Gerda watched Riley walk toward Bay. "Wait!" she shouted. "I'm going with you!"

Riley turned and shook his head. "I'm going alone!"

"No!" cried Gerda.

Sadie saw the look on Momma's face as she waited for Essie or Mart to speak to Gerda. When they didn't, Momma frowned slightly. She was used to obedient children.

Gerda ran back to Essie. "Ma, you tell him to take me!"

"But, Gerda, it wouldn't be safe," said Essie lamely.

"I want to go!" shouted Gerda, stamping her foot. "You make him take me!"

"Cousin Bess will have to do that," said Essie helplessly.

Momma rubbed her hands down her apron, and Sadie knew she was trying to find a way out of the problem Gerda was making.

Essie reached for Momma's hand. "Bess,

please have Riley take Gerda along. I know she feels responsible for Levi. Please, Bess."

Momma sighed. "All right. Riley, please take Gerda with you . . . And Sadie too."

Before Momma could change her mind, Sadie ran to tighten the cinch on Apple's saddle. She mounted and helped Gerda up behind her.

"You're so lucky, Sadie," said Helen to Sadie while Web said the same thing to Riley. "I want to go."

"But you can't, Helen," said Sadie. She knew Helen wanted to throw a fit and yell just like Gerda had done, but Helen quietly stepped back with Web. They knew they could never yell and stomp their feet. Momma would spank them if they did.

"You children be very careful," said Momma. "God is with you. Angels are watching over you."

Sadie was thankful for that.

"Don't get scalped," called Web as they rode away.

Sadie's head tingled, and she felt Gerda shiver.

8

Tirirak-ta-wirus

Sadie reined Apple in beside Bay at the edge of the valley where the Cass ranch lay. The hot afternoon wind blew against her. "What's wrong, Riley?" she whispered.

"Do you see Levi?" asked Gerda.

Riley pushed his hat to the back of his head and narrowed his dark eyes. His face was sun-browned and looked like smooth, fine leather. Wind whipped the loose sleeves of his light blue shirt. He touched the rifle in the boot of the saddle. "Things don't feel right," he said in a low, tense voice.

"What does that mean?" asked Gerda impatiently. She moved, and the saddle creaked.

"Somebody hitched up Cotton Twyll's wagon," said Riley.

Sadie gasped. She saw the team and covered wagon, with Cotton Twyll's stuff hanging neatly on

75

the outside the way it had before his team had run
away. The water barrel was roped in place with the
bucket hanging under the wagon in its usual spot.
"Maybe Joshua Cass is home and is taking care of
it," she said finally.

"Could be," said Riley, "but it doesn't feel like
that's how it is." The hairs on the back of his neck
stood on end. "Let's ride in quietly and carefully."

Nudging Apple, Sadie said over her shoulder to
Gerda, "You have to be real quiet until we see if
everything's all right."

"You act like I couldn't be quiet if I tried,"
Gerda said stiffly. "Well, I can!"

"Do it now then!" snapped Riley, scowling at
Gerda.

She clamped her mouth closed and clung to
Sadie's waist. Their skirts flapped together as Apple
walked toward the ranch yard beside Bay.
Blackbirds flew across the sky. A grasshopper
landed on Sadie's leg, but jumped right back off.

Cotton's team of horses shook their harness,
and Sadie jumped. She watched the house, but the
door didn't burst open as usual. Where were Lost
Sand Cherry and Levi?

"I don't like this a bit," said Riley as he slipped
his rifle out.

"Levi!" shouted Gerda.

"Quiet!" snapped Riley and Sadie at the same
time.

Sadie slapped Gerda's leg. "You said you'd be
quiet."

"But maybe he's inside and just didn't hear
us." Suddenly Gerda jumped from the saddle and
ran toward the house. Over her shoulder she said,
"I'm going to see if he's here. Maybe that Indian
squaw will know where he is."

Her heart in her mouth, Sadie leaped to the ground, leaving Apple's reins dangling, then raced after Gerda. They reached the front door at the same time. Before Sadie could stop her, Gerda threw open the door and stepped inside.

"Levi! Cherry! Anyone here?"

Sadie groaned, pushed her suddenly too-warm bonnet off her head to settle between her shoulder blades, and followed Gerda inside. No fire burned in the kitchen range, and everything was clean and tidy. It was almost time to start supper, but where was Lost Sand Cherry? Something was wrong! Cotton's team was hitched and ready, but no one was around. Had the Indian warrior caught Levi and Lost Sand Cherry and scalped them?

Gerda banged open both bedroom doors, then stamped her foot hard. "Where is Levi?"

"We'll check the barn and the yard," said Sadie, trembling so hard she could hardly walk. She stopped just outside the door on the porch. Bay and Apple weren't standing by the wagon. And Riley was gone! Sadie's stomach cramped.

"Where's Riley?" asked Gerda impatiently. "Did he ride off without us?" She stomped down the steps. "Riley, where are you?"

Sadie looked toward the pasture in back of the barn, but couldn't see anything except a few chickens scratching in the grass. The windmill whirred, pumping icy water through the pipe into the big wooden tank. Cotton's team of horses moved restlessly.

"I'm going to look in the barn," said Gerda, running toward the sod barn on the other side of the wagon. Just as she started past the wagon a bronze arm snaked out and caught her around the neck, cutting off a scream. The warrior had caught her!

Fear pricked Sadie's skin as she stared in horror at the Indian. No war paint covered his bronze skin now. His single bunch of hair flopped down one side of his head. He wore a vest with blue U.S. cavalry pants and high moccasins. With one deft movement he twisted Gerda's hands behind her back and tied them together with a strip of rawhide. Gerda hung limply as if she were dead.

Suddenly Sadie realized she had to get away and get help. She leaped off the porch and began running away from the wagon and away from the Cass ranch. Her braids flew out straight behind her, and her skirts bounced around her thin legs. She ran like she had run when she'd beat all the school kids at a footrace back in Douglas County. Not even the big eighth-grade boys could catch her. Now she ran like the wind along the base of a low hill, then around it. She longed to look behind her to see if the warrior was following her, but she knew she didn't dare look back and lose her stride. Once she was far enough away she could hide in the tall grass, then try to find her way back to the Circle Y for help.

Pain stabbed her side, but she kept running, her arms pumping, her head up. How she wanted to look back over her shoulder!

Suddenly a hand grabbed her and brought her up short. She stumbled and collapsed to the ground. The Indian dropped down beside her. She gasped for air, but he breathed as easily as if he hadn't chased her all that way. Grass scratched her face and arms. A bee buzzed around her head, then flew away.

"You run like the deer," the Indian said in admiration.

"Don't . . . scalp . . . me," Sadie gasped.

"I will not scalp you," he said, shaking his head. He sounded educated. "You catch your breath, and we will run back. I will like running beside such a fleet-footed girl."

Sadie stared at him. He didn't act as if he was going to harm her. Should she be frightened of him, or should she look at him as a friend? But he had caught and tied Gerda! Maybe he'd done the same with the others. Sadie shied away from him. "What will you do with me?"

"Take you to the wagon where the others wait." He stood and pulled her up beside him. He towered over her and smelled of dust and sweat. "Is the pain in your side gone?"

She nodded.

He grunted and motioned for her to run.

She bit her bottom lip to hold back a cry of despair and ran back toward the Cass ranch. The Indian easily stayed at her side.

Back at the ranch he gave her a dipper of water from the well and let her drink, and then he drank. He hung the dipper back in place, then caught her arm and walked her to the back of the wagon. She peered inside and gasped. The others were tied and gagged and sitting among Cotton Twyll's goods. Sadie saw the anguish in Lost Sand Cherry's eyes and the anger in Riley's. Gerda looked frightened and Levi hopeless.

The Indian quickly bound Sadie's wrists behind her back, easily hoisted her into the wagon, then bound her ankles. He didn't gag her, but instead ungagged the others.

Lost Sand Cherry said, "Please, Good One, let us go. Don't do this terrible thing."

"Will you decide in my favor, Lost Sand Cherry?" asked the Indian.

"I am married to Joshua Cass," she said.

Sadie gaped at the two Indians. They seemed to know each other.

"What do you plan to do with us?" asked Riley grimly. He felt bad about being caught. It galled him to think the Indian had knocked him off Bay and had caught and bound him before he could put up any kind of fight.

The Indian glanced at Riley, but didn't answer him. He jumped easily to the ground and disappeared.

"Who is he, Lost Sand Cherry?" asked Sadie, squirming until she felt more comfortable. She sat between Lost Sand Cherry and Riley and across from Gerda and Levi. There was barely enough room for them to sit among the neatly packed goods.

Lost Sand Cherry lifted her chin a fraction. "He is my brother."

"Your brother!" cried Gerda.

Levi stared in shock at Lost Sand Cherry. "Your brother? Pa said you had no family."

"He is all I have, and he was sent to a reservation in Oklahoma. The law said I did not have to go because I belonged to Reagon Leever." Her voice took on a sharp edge. "Your pa took me from that terrible man, married me, and brought me to his ranch."

Just then the wagon swayed, and Sadie saw that the Indian warrior had climbed onto the high red and gold seat. He slapped the reins against the team and urged them ahead. The wagon lurched, and Sadie almost fell over, then caught her balance.

"Where is he taking us?" asked Gerda with a sob.

"He has not told me," said Lost Sand Cherry. "Good One is keeping his plans to himself."

"Is his name really 'Good One'?" asked Sadie. It sure didn't suit him!

"His name is Tirirak-ta-wirus," said Lost Sand Cherry. "It means 'rescuer' or 'the good one who comes forward in time of need.' I have always called him Good One. I have not seen him since he was a boy."

"Does he hate you?" asked Sadie.

Lost Sand Cherry shook her head. "He thinks he is helping me by making me leave the white man's ways. He says he will find a special place for us and that I will be thankful he rescued me."

"And will you?" asked Levi coldly.

Lost Sand Cherry looked him squarely in the eyes and finally he ducked his head.

"We will all die, won't we?" whispered Gerda as she leaned heavily against Levi. "I wish we'd stayed in Michigan! But Pa was so sure we'd get rich if we moved here where he could build houses. Oh, I hate him!"

Levi frowned. "Don't blame your pa for this. It's *her* fault!" He nodded toward Lost Sand Cherry.

A hurt look fleetingly crossed Lost Sand Cherry's face before she masked it. She leaned her head back and closed her eyes, shutting out the others.

"That's not fair, Levi," snapped Sadie.

"It doesn't do any good to blame each other," said Riley. "We have to find a way to escape. And we have to do it soon."

"Do you know what he plans to do with us?" asked Levi.

Riley nodded slightly. He'd lost his hat, and a bruise covered the side of his face. "If he wanted to scalp us, he would've already done that. He has a purpose for us."

Sadie leaned forward to hear Riley over the rattle and creak of the wagon.

"I read about the Pawnee," said Riley. "They sold captives as slaves. I think Good One is planning to sell us as slaves."

Sadie gasped, and Gerda burst into tears.

Lost Sand Cherry nodded. "You are probably right," she said. "He is trying to be the proud Pawnee warrior of yesteryear."

"Pa would've stopped him," said Levi gruffly.

"So would Caleb," said Riley.

"But now it's up to us," said Sadie, sounding braver than she felt. Just how could they get away before they were sold as slaves?

"What can we do?" asked Gerda with a whimper.

"We can hold on until Joshua Cass finds us," said Sadie. "He's the best tracker around." She looked right at Levi.

Levi bit his lip, then said, "Pa knows Cotton Twyll's wagon tracks. He won't see any reason to follow them."

"But Cotton is buried at your place with a marker on his grave," said Riley. He'd helped put it there himself.

"Good One took the marker away," said Lost Sand Cherry. "He made Levi and me fix up the wagon like Cotton had it, so nobody would be suspicious if they saw it." She shook her head. "No,

Joshua will not follow Cotton Twyll's wagon to look for us."

"Caleb might see the wagon and stop Cotton to ask if he's seen us," said Riley hopefully.

"Good One will not let anyone approach the wagon until we are many miles from here and he knows it is safe," said Lost Sand Cherry.

Everyone was quiet as the wagon swayed and creaked its way away from the Nebraska sandhills.

"We can't give up," said Sadie, forcing back a sob. But in her heart she was afraid she already had. She closed her eyes before the others spotted her tears and leaned her head against the side of the wagon.

9
Arguments

Sadie woke with a start. Her stomach ached with hunger, and she had to use the toilet. For a minute she couldn't place where she was. She knew it wasn't in the bed she shared with Opal and Helen. Sadie heard a groan and a whimper. Then she remembered. She was a captive along with Lost Sand Cherry, Gerda, Riley, and Levi!

Suddenly the wagon stopped. The silence was so great that it seemed to hurt Sadie's ears. Then she heard the night sounds of bugs and frogs that she knew lived only near water. In the distance coyotes yapped. A horse nickered, and it sounded so much like Apple that Sadie started to cry. She had been afraid to think of what Good One had done to Apple, Bay, and Netty.

Just then Good One opened the flap at the back of the wagon and let down the tailgate.

Moonlight flooded in. "Get out to stretch your legs and eat," he said.

Sadie inched her way to the back, and Good One lifted her down, untied her ankles and wrists, then shackled her wrists in front of her so she was still bound but could use her hands. The rawhide string between her wrists was about twelve inches long and gave her limited freedom. Oh, but it felt good to stand!

Sadie heard water running in the creek beside them and listened to the night birds and insects. She saw a movement at the side of the wagon. As her eyes grew more accustomed to the dimness, she realized Good One had tied Bay, Apple, and Netty to the wagon. "Apple," whispered Sadie.

Apple nickered, and Sadie felt better.

Soon the others stood beside Sadie at the sandy bank of the creek. All of them were shackled except Lost Sand Cherry.

"See that they eat," said Good One gruffly. With a quick look around he walked off into the darkness.

"I want to go home," whimpered Gerda. "Levi, make him let me go."

"Nobody can make him," said Riley.

Gerda stamped her foot hard, sending sand spraying out around her. "I want to go home right now!"

"It won't do any good to throw a fit," said Riley impatiently. "Good One won't give in, no matter what you do."

"Leave me alone, Riley York," snapped Gerda. "I wasn't talking to you!"

"He's right though," said Levi. "We can't get away."

"Where do you think we are, Levi?" asked Riley.

"Heading south," Levi said. "If he keeps going we'll be at the North Loup River tomorrow sometime."

Sadie didn't know where the North Loup River was, but by the sound of Levi's voice she decided she never wanted to reach it. She wanted to go home!

Later Good One ordered Lost Sand Cherry to find blankets for them from Cotton's supplies. He tied each of them to a wheel, but allowed Lost Sand Cherry to sleep inside the wagon. Trembling, Sadie settled down in her blanket against the front left wheel. She heard Riley and Levi whispering on the other side of the wagon. Were they planning a get-away? Sadie shook her head slightly. Probably they were tied as securely as she was, and that meant they couldn't get away unless they somehow took whole wheels with them.

Gerda leaned against the wheel she was tied to and wept. Good One was fast asleep under a tree, with the horses staked nearby. Inside the wagon Lost Sand Cherry moved restlessly.

"I hate this," said Gerda between sobs.

"We all do," said Sadie, trying to get comfortable. She was tired of being angry and frightened. She wanted to be home in her own bed with Helen crowding her and Opal jerking the quilt off her each time she turned over.

"I hate it more because I'm not a country person," said Gerda hoarsely. "I never ever slept on the ground."

"Just roll up in your blanket and go to sleep," said Riley impatiently.

Gerda cried harder, and Sadie tried to block out the sound.

Finally Sadie fell asleep and was awakened at the crack of dawn by Good One shaking her shoulder. He wore Cotton Twyll's bowler hat, a blue shirt, and heavy denims that were part of Cotton's supplies. Worn moccasins were still on his feet. He didn't look like a warrior at all. Part of Sadie's fear of him trickled away.

"Get up. Help Sand Cherry make breakfast," said Good One as he untied her from the wheel, leaving her hands shackled.

Shivering from the chilly wind that blew through her wrinkled dirty dress, Sadie struggled to her feet. She saw Gerda curled in a ball against her wheel, the blanket tight around her. Sadie awkwardly pushed her tangled hair out of her face as she walked toward the campfire and Lost Sand Cherry.

Lost Sand Cherry glanced up, frowned at Good One, and tired to smile at Sadie. Her eyes were smudged, and she looked as if she hadn't slept. "I am sorry for what my brother is doing," she said.

Sadie didn't know what to say to make Lost Sand Cherry feel better. "It's not your fault."

"No talk!" barked Good One. "Cook the food."

Anger flashed across Lost Sand Cherry's face, but she quickly masked it and handed Sadie a long wooden spoon. "Stir the mush. I will check the biscuits."

Good One tapped the bowler hat tighter on his head and walked to the wagon.

Sadie stood over the black kettle hanging from a tripod over the fire. Cornmeal and water bubbled together. Sadie stirred it, flinching at the heat from the fire.

Lost Sand Cherry pulled a heavy container out of the fire, lifted the lid, and looked inside at the biscuits. The smell rose up around them, and Sadie realized how hungry she was. "They are done," said Lost Sand Cherry.

Several minutes later Sadie sat between Riley and Good One and ate mush and biscuits. They sat in a circle around the fire to keep back the chill of the dawn. Even Gerda ate without complaining.

When everything was packed away and the campfire covered with sand and the team harnessed, Good One ordered them to climb back into the wagon. He bound their ankles and retied their hands behind their backs, then climbed onto the seat and slapped the reins against the horses.

Sadie wrinkled her nose at the smell of sweaty bodies and the smoke from the campfire that clung to her. It was hard to see in the dimness after the bright daylight outdoors.

"He don't dare let us be seen walkin'," said Levi. "Somebody might recognize us. But once we're past the North Loup where we're not known, he'll make us walk."

Sadie shivered. Now she had another reason for not wanting to reach the North Loup River.

"Walkin' will be better than this," said Riley, trying to get comfortable.

"Being home is better than this," snapped Gerda, jerking so hard she bumped her head on the side of the wagon. She burst into tears and wailed at the top of her lungs.

Sadie kicked Gerda's foot and said, "Stop it! Do you want Good One to come back here and gag us again?"

Gerda's cry died in her throat. "You didn't have

to kick me," she said, kicking out at Sadie. She missed and hit Riley in the calf of the leg.

He flung his body forward and almost knocked Lost Sand Cherry over. "Keep away from me, Gerda Tasker! You got us into this, and I'm on the verge of knockin' you out the back of this wagon for coyote bait!"

"Riley!" cried Sadie. She'd never heard him talk that way to anyone, not even Web when he'd pushed Riley beyond endurance with all his questions and teasing and wrestling.

Levi rammed his boot against Riley. "Stop it, Riley York! Leave Gerda alone. She's not used to our way of livin'."

"She's not used to actin' like a nice person," said Riley grimly. "I'm sure sorry she's a cousin to us."

"So am I!" said Sadie. "I hate you, Gerda Tasker!" The ugly words hung in the air, and Sadie wanted to grab them back. How could she have said such a naughty thing?

"Children," said Lost Sand Cherry softly. "Please listen to me."

"No! . . . Don't listen to her!" growled Levi, glaring at her.

Lost Sand Cherry turned to Levi with a stern look on her face. "You will listen, and so will the others! Sit back and be quiet!"

With a surprised look Levi sank back.

Gerda started to speak, but Lost Sand Cherry stopped her with a piercing look from her dark eyes.

Sadie trembled and sat quietly. The rawhide cut into her wrists, and she winced.

"This arguing must stop," said Lost Sand Cherry. "We are in enough trouble without adding strife to it. Sadie, Riley, and you too, Levi, know the Scripture 'Where there is envy and strife, there is confusion and every evil work.' We must not add to our problems by having strife among us."

Sadie hung her head. Momma had often quoted that Scripture to remind all of them to be kind and to live in harmony together in the small confines of the sod house.

"We need God with us to help us," continued Lost Sand Cherry. "He can't help us if we are setting every evil work into motion by our strife. He will not be able to help us find a way out of our trouble if we are full of confusion."

For a while the only sounds were the creak of the wagon and the rattle of the harness. Finally Riley said, "I'm sorry, everyone. Gerda, I am sorry. Please forgive me."

"Forgive me too," whispered Sadie.

Gerda sniffed and tossed her head. "I don't know why I should, but I guess I will."

"And now we will pray," said Lost Sand Cherry, bowing her head.

Sadie prayed silently as Lost Sand Cherry prayed aloud for forgiveness, protection, and help to get home again.

"And comfort the hearts of our loved ones who will be afraid for us," prayed Lost Sand Cherry.

After several minutes of silence Levi said, "Pa's supposed to get home today. What will he think about the fresh grave and us being gone?"

"He is a strong man of God," said Lost Sand Cherry. "He will trust God to show him what to do."

"Daddy too," whispered Sadie. Caleb always listened to God. Caleb would know what to do.

"Us too!" Riley said with a ring of triumph in

his voice. "We will trust God to show us what to do!"

Sadie's heart leaped. "That's right," she said.

10

The Broken Wheel

A fly buzzed around Sadie's tangled hair, and she jerked her head to avoid it. "That dumb fly!" she cried. She was hot and dirty and hungry again. She knew it was past noon, but Good One had stopped only long enough for the horses to drink, then pushed on. Lost Sand Cherry had begged him to lift the back flap to let in fresh air, but he had refused.

Suddenly the wagon swayed and the back right axle hit the ground with a thud. Sadie flew back toward the low corner, and the supplies and the others rolled after her, almost smothering her. She struggled, but couldn't move. "Get off me," she said, but her voice was muffled against a pile of dusty blankets.

"I'm squashed!" cried Gerda, jerking to free herself.

"Whoever is on top, roll off," said Lost Sand

Cherry. Before anyone could move, Good One opened the flap and lifted out the endgate. He pulled each one out roughly, leaving them in a heap on the ground. "White boys, get up and help me fix the wheel," he said gruffly.

Sadie rolled out of the tangled blanket and tried to stand. But she couldn't with her ankles and wrists still bound. Helplessly she sat in the tall grass and watched as Good One untied Riley and Levi.

"Good One," said Lost Sand Cherry from where she lay on the ground, "untie me and I will get water for all of us."

At the thought of water Sadie's mouth suddenly felt bone-dry. But she knew the water in the barrel would be lukewarm, and she longed for a icy cold drink straight from the well of the Circle Y.

Good One hesitated, then untied Lost Sand Cherry. He helped her to her feet and brushed sand off her skirts. "Are you ready to come willingly with me?" he asked softly.

"I belong with Joshua Cass," she said just as softly. "I love him. I love you too, Good One. I will always remember our days together when you were a small boy. But I will not go with you in hopes that the Pawnee tribe will once again become great. It is too late for that."

Good One's face hardened. "I will not give up! Before the white man, before the white man's disease, we were a great nation! We must become a great nation again!"

Lost Sand Cherry gently touched Good One's face. "No, my brother. It cannot be. No matter how much you will it to be, it cannot be."

Abruptly Good One turned away and hauled Riley and Levi up and shoved them toward the broken-down wagon. The hubnut was gone, and the wheel had slipped off.

Riley glanced at Levi, then looked around for the lost hubnut. Sadie learned later that Riley and Levi had planned the breakdown. During the night Riley had worked on the hubnut until it was loose and would work itself off when the wagon began moving. He'd thought it would happen earlier in the day, not during the hottest part of the afternoon.

Suddenly Levi leaped away from the wagon and ran to Netty, untied her in one easy motion, and sprang onto her back. He leaned low on her neck and sent her galloping across the prairie toward several uneven hills.

"Stop!" shouted Good One. He reached for the rifle that he'd leaned against the wagon and took aim, but before he could fire Riley knocked the rifle upward, wasting the shot on empty air. Good One swung the rifle and cracked Riley across the jaw. Riley dropped in a heap to the ground.

Sadie cried out, frustrated to tears that she couldn't go to her brother. "Did you kill him?" she cried.

"He is alive," said Good One angrily. "But if the boy Levi does not return, I will kill this one."

"No!" screamed Sadie. "I'll go after Levi . . . I'll bring him back!"

"Let him get away," snapped Gerda. "He'll bring help for us."

Lost Sand Cherry knelt beside Riley and lifted his head. He moaned and slowly sat up. Lost Sand Cherry looked angrily up at Good One. "You could have killed him!"

"I *will* kill him if Levi does not return."

Sadie rocked back and forth, trying to scoot

toward the Indian. She knew Good One meant just what he said. "Untie me . . . I can get Levi back."

"Let him go, Sadie," said Riley. "He's our only hope."

"I will kill you," said Good One, sticking the rifle in Riley's face.

"Then I will die!" Riley's voice rang out. "I will die before I let you sell my sister as a slave!"

Sadie shook her head hard. "No! No, Riley! I don't want you to die!"

Good One narrowed his eyes. "Lost Sand Cherry, untie the small girl who runs like the deer. She will bring back Levi."

"Don't do it!" shouted Gerda.

Lost Sand Cherry sighed and untied Sadie. Good One had Apple ready and boosted Sadie up. She clung to Apple with her knees. She'd ridden without a saddle many times. She held the reins and shouted to Apple.

Apple galloped after Levi as if she knew what Sadie wanted of her. Caleb had always said Apple was the best cow pony in the sandhills of Nebraska.

Wind whipped Sadie's hair and dress and felt like it would whip her off Apple, but Sadie clung like a sandbur. She spotted Levi just before he disappeared around a hill. "Levi!" she called at the top of her lungs. "Levi, come back!" The words seemed to be flung back in her face, but she shouted again. She reached the hill Levi had ridden around and followed it. She caught a glimpse of Levi and knew Apple could catch Netty even though she'd had such a long head start.

Apple ran faster, as if her hooves weren't even touching the ground. Sadie saw the distance between Apple and Netty growing narrower. "Levi!" Sadie shouted again and again.

Finally Levi glanced back, saw Sadie on Apple, and slowed Netty. Levi's heart thudded painfully. How had Sadie gotten away? He turned Netty and rode toward Sadie. They reined in together. "Are you free too?" he asked.

Sadie gasped for breath. Her face felt on fire from the hot wind. "Levi, you have to go back with me," she said, breathing hard.

"No!"

"Good One will shoot Riley if I don't bring you back." Sadie's face crumpled.

"Lost Sand Cherry will stop him."

"She can't! I said I would take you back."

"I won't go!"

"Oh, Levi! . . . You have to!"

Levi's shoulders slumped, and he reached across and patted Sadie's arm. "I know. At least I tried to get away." He grinned shakily.

Sadie nodded. "You tried. I just wish it would've worked."

"Next time," said Levi with a nod. "Next time!"

Several minutes later they rode up to the wagon. The wheel was back in place. Riley and Gerda were tied in the shade of the wagon. With Lost Sand Cherry beside him Good One sat nearby, the rifle across his knees.

"Levi!" cried Gerda, holding her arms out as Levi slid off Netty. Gerda wanted to go to Levi, but she could only move as far as the rope would let her.

Sadie dropped to the ground and ran to Riley.

"I will kill you!" roared Good One, aiming the rifle right at Levi.

"No!" cried Lost Sand Cherry, gripping his arm. "No, Tirirak-ta-wirus, you cannot!"

He glared at her. "I will kill him!"

Lost Sand Cherry shook her head. "No!"

"He is trouble for me."

"Don't kill him!" begged Lost Sand Cherry.

"He has been trouble for you."

Levi's face turned as white as the clouds in the bright blue sky. His legs trembled, but he locked his knees and wouldn't let the others see how frightened he was. He knew he really had been trouble for Lost Sand Cherry ever since she'd married his pa.

"You can't kill him," said Sadie in alarm. "I promised to bring him back so you wouldn't kill Riley. I kept my word."

Lost Sand Cherry stepped between Levi and Good One. "If you shoot him, then you must shoot me first."

"Move aside, Lost Sand Cherry," said Good One hoarsely.

"I will not let you kill Levi Cass. He is family to me."

Levi stared at Lost Sand Cherry. How could she protect him after he'd been so mean to her?

Good One caught Lost Sand Cherry's arm and jerked her aside. "I must kill him!"

Sadie gasped, and Gerda screamed.

"If you do, you will no longer be my brother." Lost Sand Cherry lifted her chin and stood with her fists doubled at her sides. "Tirirak-ta-wirus, I will rip you out of my heart. That is my promise to you."

Sadie held her breath. She felt the struggle inside Good One.

Gerda bit her lip, but for once didn't speak.

Good One kept the rifle aimed at Levi for a long time, then slowly lowered it. "He can have his life."

"Thank you," said Lost Sand Cherry.

Levi sagged in relief as he wiped sweat from his face.

Sadie touched Lost Sand Cherry's arm and smiled. "Thank you."

Lost Sand Cherry looked at Levi as if she were waiting for something, then turned away.

Sadie jabbed Levi and whispered, "Tell her thank you."

Levi ducked his head. He couldn't talk around the lump in his throat. Was it possible that Lost Sand Cherry really cared for him?

Sadie slipped her arm around Lost Sand Cherry's waist and just stood there with her.

11

The North Loup River

From the high point of the hill Sadie looked down and saw the ribbon of water. Her heart sank. She knew before Levi said anything that she was looking at the North Loup River. Once they crossed the river no one would know Levi Cass or recognize his mare Netty. No one would wonder why York's mares, Bay and Apple, were tied to a peddler's wagon.

Sadie leaned weakly against the wagon and waited while Good One forced the others into the back and retied their hands and feet. The cornbread and beans she'd eaten a few minutes earlier lay heavy on her stomach. Dragonflies darted among a bunch of blue wildflowers. A bumblebee landed on a blossom, sat there a minute, and flew away. If she were seeing those wildflowers at home, she'd pick a bouquet for Momma. "Oh, Momma," whispered Sadie.

Good One motioned to Sadie, and she crept inside the wagon and waited for him to bind her ankles and wrists. Tears burned her eyes while the hot sun burned down on the covered wagon.

"The North Loup River," said Levi with a deep sigh as Good One slapped the reins on the team.

"We can still get away," said Riley in a strong, firm voice. "We can't give up!"

Sadie leaned her head back and closed her eyes while the wagon swayed and bounced down the hill to the North Loup River.

Gerda moaned and moved restlessly. "I'm so hot!" she whimpered.

"We're all hot," said Sadie tiredly.

Gerda swayed until she was leaning against Levi. "I don't feel good," she said weakly.

Levi felt her burning skin through his shirt. "She is hot! I think she has a fever."

"I don't feel good," Gerda whimpered again.

"Lost Sand Cherry, what can we do?" asked Levi. Suddenly he realized he'd asked for her help in a polite manner for the first time ever. He flushed. Would she notice?

"I will try to get Good One to stop," she said quietly. She turned her head toward the sunlight filtering through the front of the wagon. "Good One!" she called. "Good One, please stop the wagon!"

But the wagon continued to roll toward the North Loup River. Either Good One had not heard or he was simply refusing to stop.

"I am sorry," said Lost Sand Cherry. "When we stop at the river I will see to Gerda."

"Thank you," said Levi, flushing with embarrassment. He was glad it was too dark for the others to see his red neck and face.

The closed-in smell inside the wagon turned

Sadie's stomach. She tried to block out Gerda's moans, but they seemed to echo across the wagon and inside her head. She wanted to tell Gerda to be quiet, but she knew she shouldn't. She hesitated, then silently prayed for Gerda, then for all of them.

Suddenly she realized the wagon had slowed. Was Good One going to stop after all? She tensed, listening intently for any new sounds. Finally she heard running water above the sounds of Gerda's moans and groans. The North Loup River! Sadie closed her eyes and bit her bottom lip to hold back a cry of agony.

She heard water splash and felt the wagon wheels sink as they rolled into the river. She knew they all realized they were crossing the river, but no one said a word.

The wagon moved slower and slower, then stopped. Good One shouted to the team and slapped the reins hard on their backs. One of the horses neighed shrilly, and the wagon swayed but didn't move.

Sadie held her breath and waited. "What's wrong?" she whispered.

"We're bogged down," said Riley weakly.

"What does that mean?" whispered Gerda, lifting her head from Levi's arm.

"We're stuck in the river," said Lost Sand Cherry softly.

Sadie knew from their trip from Douglas County to the Circle Y Ranch that such an event could mean lost goods or a lost wagon or even a lost life.

"Maybe the wagon is stuck, but with work we can get it out," said Riley.

Apple whinnied, and Netty answered. Then all was quiet except a crane's call and the lap of water under the wagon.

Good One crawled through the front of the wagon. Cotton's bowler fell off the Indian's head, and he left it where it lay beside the hats that Sadie admired so much.

"Untie us and we will help you," said Lost Sand Cherry.

Good One grunted and untied Lost Sand Cherry first, then went to Riley.

Lost Sand Cherry flung the back flap open and let in fresh air and sunlight.

Good One said, "I will hold the one who talks too much on the seat with me." He looked right at Gerda, and she cringed. "If anyone runs away I will kill her."

Gerda gasped. "Don't any of you dare try to run away! Levi, do you hear me?"

"Yes," he said impatiently.

Soon everyone except Gerda was untied. Good One lashed her to the high red and gold seat, and she immediately burst into tears.

Good One motioned for the others to climb out the back into the water. Sadie hesitated, then eased herself down into the muddy water. It felt warm on her legs. Her skirts billowed up around her and floated on the water. Flushing, she pushed them down until they were wet and would stay down.

She waded a few steps from the wagon and looked from one bank to the other. The river wasn't very wide, and the water looked shallow, no more than waist deep. A few willows and cottonwoods lined the banks. She could see Good One had chosen this spot to cross because both banks were free of trees, making it easy for a wagon to go in and out. Caleb had said never to trust a river. Good One must not have tested it.

"Riley, Levi, and Sadie, saddle your mares," said Good One. "With the team and the mares pulling together, we can get out. The wagon is bogged down, but the team is not."

Several minutes later Sadie, on Apple, looped the rope that Riley had tied to the front axle around the saddle horn and waited for the signal. Her wet skirts felt heavy on her legs. Water sloshed in her shoes. The afternoon sun burned down on her head and shoulders. She glanced at Lost Sand Cherry on the far bank. Levi had taken her across on Netty to check the river bottom. He'd said it was safe.

Apple bobbed her head and nickered. Sadie patted Apple's neck. "Easy, girl. We'll be out of here soon."

"Ready," called Riley, taking his place between Sadie and Levi. The three mares led the way with ropes hooked to the axle. The team and wagon were close behind them.

"Pull!" shouted Good One, gripping the reins as he slapped them against the team.

Sadie felt the jerk against the saddle as Apple stepped forward, straining against the weight of the wagon. Sadie felt Apple's muscles bunch as she tried to step forward. "Keep tryin', Apple," whispered Sadie. She could hear Riley talking to Bay and Levi to Netty. Good One shouted at the team, his voice loud in the great silence of the prairie.

Suddenly the wagon came loose, and the horses leaped forward. Sadie glanced back to see muddy water boiling around the wagon wheels. They were free! "Yahoo!" shouted Sadie, waving her arm high as Apple kept a steady pace toward dry land.

"We made it!" shouted Riley while Levi let out a loud cowboy yell.

On land Sadie let the rope fall from her saddle horn and rode Apple out of the way of the wagon.

If she wanted, she could ride like the wind for help. She watched Gerda swaying on the wagon, shook her head, and groaned. She couldn't leave.

Good One stopped the wagon beside Lost Sand Cherry, and she smiled up at him.

"Good work!" shouted Levi as he leaped down to loosen the ropes from the axle.

The rifle in his hand, Good One stood up and started to step to the side of the high seat to climb down. Suddenly Gerda kicked him on the leg, sending him off balance. The rifle flew from his hand. With a cry Good One flipped backwards and landed with a loud thud near the left front wheel, several feet from the rifle.

Sadie sprang to the ground and scooped up the rifle. Butterflies fluttered in her stomach as she aimed it at the warrior.

Levi leaped on Good One, but the Indian threw him off easily.

Gerda screamed.

"Sadie, don't shoot him!" cried Lost Sand Cherry.

As Riley rode up on Bay, he eased out a loop and swung the rope just like Caleb had taught him to do. The rope sailed through the air and landed over Good One, pinning his arms to his sides. Just as Riley knew she would, Bay jumped to tighten the rope, and Good One sprawled to the muddy ground.

Her heart in her mouth, Sadie shouted, "Don't move, Good One. I have the rifle on you!" Would the Pawnee warrior find a way to get free and in his anger kill them all?

Lost Sand Cherry ran to Good One's side. "Don't fight, Good One," she begged. "Let us go!"

Good One jumped up, then twisted and turned like a wild man, but Bay backed enough each time to keep the rope tight. Finally Riley nudged Bay back even further until Good One fell to the ground again. "Get his feet, Levi," called Riley.

"Be careful, Levi!" screamed Gerda.

With a rope in his hand Levi ran toward Good One. The Indian kicked out, and Levi jumped back.

Gerda screamed again.

Riley backed Bay up another step, dragging Good One so he couldn't kick. The team moved nervously, jangling their harness.

Seeing his chance, Levi leaped on Good One and twisted a rope around his ankles and legs, then up around where Riley's rope was. Levi had moved as fast as he'd ever done on the range during branding.

"Shoot him, Sadie!" called Gerda.

Sadie's grip tightened, but she knew she wouldn't shoot unless she was forced to.

Lost Sand Cherry looked beseechingly at Sadie and the boys. "Please do not hurt him."

Levi stepped back, and Riley jumped to the ground, letting Bay hold the rope tight on her own.

"Levi, get me down!" called Gerda.

"We got him," said Levi, grinning at Riley.

Riley nodded.

"I saved us," called Gerda. "I saved us all!"

"I guess she did," said Riley in surprise.

Sadie pressed her lips tightly together and didn't say anything.

"Levi!" called Gerda.

Levi climbed up on the wagon, untied Gerda, and helped her to the ground. He gave her a drink of water and watched while she splashed water on her face.

Sadie gritted her teeth and turned away from Gerda and Levi. She was glad they were free, but how she hated to think Gerda had done it.

"Levi, bring water," said Lost Sand Cherry.

Sadie stood back as Lost Sand Cherry knelt beside Good One. His face was muddy, and his eyes flashed with anger. "Is he all right?" asked Sadie.

"Yes," said Lost Sand Cherry. "He needs a drink."

"What will we do with him?" asked Sadie.

"Send him back to the reservation," said Riley.

"I will die before I go back there!"

Levi handed Lost Sand Cherry the dipper of water. "Pa will send him right back," Levi said gruffly.

Good One jerked, but he was tied too securely to move much.

"Lie still and let me clean you," said Lost Sand Cherry.

Riley looked back across the North Loup River. "Now we have to cross back over," he said quietly.

Sadie took a deep breath. "But we'll make it! We have to, Riley."

Gerda jabbed Sadie's arm. "Aren't you going to thank me for saving your life?"

Sadie's face turned brick-red. "Thank you," she said, almost choking on the words.

Gerda beamed, then turned to Riley. "Well?"

"Thank you," he said with a grin. He still couldn't believe she'd had the courage to kick Good One. Maybe she wouldn't be such a bad cousin after all.

Gerda turned back to Sadie. "I need another drink. Get me one, will you? I *am* sick, you know."

Sadie wanted to refuse, but she handed the rifle to Riley and ran to the water barrel.

12
Good One's Story

Sadie curled in her blanket close to the campfire. She knew Gerda was asleep inside the wagon. She'd chosen to ride there since she wasn't feeling well. Sadie had been glad to be astride Apple with the wind blowing against her. Since Good One's capture they'd traveled as far as they could, but had been forced to stop when darkness fell. Levi had said it was safer, and he knew best.

Riley and Levi lay a couple of feet away, rolled in their blankets. Lost Sand Cherry still sat up talking with Good One, who was securely bound.

Sadie closed her eyes and tried not to eavesdrop, but she could hear them easily over the occasional crackle of the fire and the low murmur of the creek they'd camped beside.

"I will not go back," Good One said for the hundredth time since they'd overpowered him. "Give me a knife and I will cut out my heart. I will not go back."

"Is it that bad?" asked Lost Sand Cherry sadly.

"It is bad. Remember when I was young, the winter we had no food but a rancher's beef?"

"I remember."

Sadie bit her lip. She had been hungry a few times, but never had she come close to starving.

"Most of my days on the reservation were like that. I married Lone Deer two summers ago. She had a son for me. But there was no food."

"The government gave their word to supply food, Good One."

"They did not keep their word. Lone Deer was weak and could not nurse my son. He died. Lone Deer became sick." Good One's voice broke slightly. "She died. That is when I knew it was time for me to become a Pawnee warrior again, not a sick man living in a land that belonged to another. We had land . . . land that belongs to our people. I will take back that land. I came to rescue you . . . so you could be Pawnee. That is our destiny."

"I am Pawnee," said Lost Sand Cherry gently, "but I am wife to Joshua Cass too. If you were free to leave here, I would not go with you. I belong with Joshua Cass. We are one."

Sadie looked at the twinkling stars above and the crackling fire nearby. How would she feel if *she* were Pawnee? Would she want all Pawnee to be free? She nodded slightly. She knew she would.

"I will speak with your Joshua Cass. I will tell him I am Pawnee. I will live on my land and plant and harvest my crops. I will not live on reservation."

Lost Sand Cherry sighed. "You talk to Joshua. He will understand. He does not feel the government had a right to take land from Pawnee or any other red man. But it is done. He will have an answer for you."

"You are not angry with me, Lost Sand Cherry?"

"I love you, Good One. I have learned to love with a pure heart. I know God, the Maker, the Provider. I will tell you what I know."

Sadie listened long into the night as brother and sister talked. Sometime during the night Sadie drifted into sleep. She woke up abruptly the next morning when she heard Riley's shout.

"Today we go home!" he called, then threw back his head and laughed.

Sadie jumped up, washed at the creek, and braided her hair. She looked at her dirty, limp bonnet and longed for the beautiful hat in the back of Cotton's wagon. She had tried it on only once in a weak moment last night, then had immediately put it away—but not before Levi had seen her. He hadn't said anything, and she was thankful for that.

After breakfast Levi and Riley hitched the team to the wagon and tied Good One on the high seat beside Lost Sand Cherry, who was driving.

"I'll ride in the back," said Gerda, looking weak and tired and dirty as she climbed in.

"Aren't you feeling better?" asked Levi from Netty's back.

"Oh, maybe a little. I want to go home," Gerda said, then disappeared inside the wagon.

Levi rode Netty alongside the wagon in case Gerda changed her mind later and wanted to ride with him.

Sadie and Riley rode ahead to lead the way. Sadie watched the sun climb in the east. Levi had said they'd be back at the Cass ranch before high noon. Mid-afternoon they'd be back at the Circle Y! Excitement bubbled inside Sadie, and she wanted to shout for Apple to run.

Several minutes later she turned to Riley. "Did you hear Lost Sand Cherry and Good One last night?"

"Yes."

"I feel sorry for him."

"Me too. But what he did to us wasn't right!"

"I know." Sadie fingered the saddle horn. "But couldn't we forgive him? Couldn't we help him find a ranch to work on? He might be happy as a cowboy."

All his life Riley had heard terrible stories about how the Indians had shed the white man's blood. Before last night he'd never thought about the rights the Indians had to the land they'd always lived on. "I don't know what to say," Riley finally said. "I reckon it's up to Joshua Cass."

Much later Gerda's call to Levi floated up to Sadie. She turned in the saddle to see Gerda slipping behind Levi on Netty. Sadie's jaw tightened. Had Gerda pretended to be sick last night and this morning just to get out of helping?

"Look!" cried Riley, pointing.

Sadie turned forward again and laughed out loud. "The Cass ranch!" With a glad cry she shouted to Apple. Apple leaped ahead and ran flatout down the valley and to the ranch yard. Chickens squawked and scattered. Sadie reined in near the well. Joshua Cass wasn't home or he would certainly be running out to greet her.

Riley stopped beside Sadie and leaped to the ground beside the large wooden tank. He splashed water on his face and neck and drank icy water from the dipper hanging at the well.

Sadie wished she could get a bar of soap and jump in the tank to wash like they often did in the tank at the Circle Y. She washed the best she could, then drank two dippers of water. "Soon we'll be home, Riley!" Tears of joy stung her eyes.

She looked over at Cotton Twyll's grave. It seemed like weeks had gone by since they'd buried him instead of just a few days. She heard Levi and Gerda riding up on Netty. Slowly Sadie turned to Riley. He was watching the wagon coming toward the ranch. "I don't want Good One sent back to the reservation," whispered Sadie.

Riley only shrugged. He still didn't know how he felt.

Suddenly a daring plan leaped into Sadie's mind. She could set Good One free so he wouldn't have to return to the reservation. "I will do it!" she said so low that only she could hear the daring words.

Later Riley fed and watered the team and put them and Netty out to pasture. Levi tied Good One to the wagon wheel while everyone went inside to eat. Riley had said he and Sadie would let Bay and Apple rest a while, and then they'd head home.

Sadie filled a plate with food, careful not to let anyone see her hands tremble. "I'll take this out to Good One," she said.

"Thank you," said Lost Sand Cherry.

Sadie carried the food to the shade of the wagon. Good One leaned against the wheel, his head and shoulders bent. A fly buzzed around his bald head and the shock of black hair. His wrists and ankles were shackled, and a rope snaked around his waist and lashed him to the wheel. "I brought you something to eat," she said.

He looked up without expression. "I will not eat."

She squatted down beside him. "If I let you go, will you promise not to hurt us or anyone else? Will you go find a place to live and be happy?"

He eyed her suspiciously. "Why would you let me go?"

"Because I don't want you sent back to the reservation. I want you to be free."

"You are a white girl."

"I know. Like Lost Sand Cherry I belong to God, the Maker, the Provider. I want you to belong to Him and learn to love and forgive and be happy." Sadie glanced toward the house. "Please eat. You need your strength."

He ate quickly, then wiped the back of his hand across his mouth and down the denim pants he'd taken from Cotton's wagon.

Sadie untied his ankles first, then his wrists. Just as she reached for the rope around his waist, the door slammed and Levi stepped out. Sadie gasped and worked faster, but the rough rope bit into her fingers and she couldn't get the knot free.

"Sadie, what're you doing?" asked Levi from behind her. Sadie glanced up at Levi, then back at the knot. "I want him free!" she hissed. "And don't try to stop me!"

"He'll kill us," snapped Levi, pulling Sadie away from Good One. Levi reached for the rope to tie Good One's wrists again, but the Indian grabbed him and held him in a death lock.

Sadie caught at Good One's hands. "Let him go! Please! You can't kill him!"

Good One loosened his hold to give Levi air, but still kept him tight against him. "All whiteskins lie!"

"No . . . I don' t lie! I want you free." Sadie tugged at the bronze arm. "Let him go."

With Levi tight against him, Good One jumped up and the rope from his waist fell at his feet. Sadie had loosened it enough that he was able to finish untying it.

Suddenly Lost Sand Cherry burst from the house, a rifle in her hands. "Let him go, Good One!" she cried. "I will shoot you if you don't!"

Levi stared at Lost Sand Cherry in surprise. She sounded like a mother protecting her young. Was it possible that she loved him like a son? The thought tore through him, leaving him weak.

Good One's dark eyes locked with Lost Sand Cherry's.

"How did he get free?" asked Riley. Sadie hadn't seen Gerda or Riley come out of the house.

Sadie swallowed hard, but kept her eyes glued to Good One. "I untied him," she said weakly.

"Sadie Rose York!" cried Riley. "What a dumb thing to do!"

"It was not!" Sadie touched Good One's muscled arm. "Letting Levi go would make you free too."

"She is right, Good One," said Lost Sand Cherry, the rifle steady against her shoulder.

Sadie held her breath and waited. Finally Good One dropped his hands to his sides. Levi leaped away to stand beside Lost Sand Cherry. She lowered the rifle, her eyes watchful.

Good One walked away from the wagon and turned south.

"Where will you go?" asked Lost Sand Cherry.

He stopped and turned to face her. "I have nowhere to go."

"Stay here," said Lost Sand Cherry. "You are family." She turned to Levi. "What do you say?"

Levi smiled. "It's up to you. You're the ma around here."

Lost Sand Cherry's dark eyes sparkled with unshed tears as she turned back to Good One. "You are welcome to stay. Joshua will also want you."

Sadie ran to Good One. "You can stay! You'll be happy here."

Good One nodded. "I will stay, Fleet Foot." He touched her hair and smiled.

13
Home Again

Just outside the sod barn at the Circle Y Sadie clung to Momma, then turned to Caleb. His arms wrapped around her so tight she thought her bones would snap. Momma had told them Opal, Web, and Helen were out on the prairie picking up cow chips, but would be back soon.

Finally Caleb held Sadie out from him and looked down into her face. "Sadie Rose, you're a sight for sore eyes," he said in his Texas drawl.

"So are you!" Sadie laughed. She was used to Caleb talking that way. And he always called her Sadie Rose, no matter how many times she said she was called only Sadie. It had taken her a while to learn to love him, but now she loved him with a love so big that it almost choked her at times.

Caleb turned to Riley and hugged him just as tight. They were both tall and strong, and both wore wide-brimmed hats and slanted high-heeled boots. Caleb carried a Colt .45 on his left hip and a bone-handled Bowie knife in a leather sheath on his right hip.

Just then Gerda's angry voice cut through Sadie's happiness. She glanced around the yard and spotted Gerda with her parents standing at the door of the tiny sod house.

Momma slipped an arm around Sadie's waist. "We have news for you," she said quietly, but she was looking at the Taskers, not at Sadie and Riley.

A shiver trickled down Sadie's back. "What news?" she whispered.

Across the yard Gerda burst into loud tears. A rooster crowed, then was quiet.

Riley pushed his hat to the back of his head and looked down at Momma. "Let's hear it," he said.

Caleb caught Momma's hand and held it. "It's somethin' we'll all have to get used to."

"What is it?" asked Sadie, suddenly frightened. She wanted to yell for Gerda to stop crying, but she knew Momma wouldn't like that.

Momma smiled, but she didn't look very happy. "Our cousins are going to live here a while."

"In the old sod house," said Caleb.

Sadie gasped and looked helplessly toward the tiny sod house. The Taskers were inside with the door shut. All the way back from the Cass ranch, with Gerda riding behind her on Apple, she'd held on to her anger at Gerda because she knew Gerda would be leaving soon. But now she was going to live in the tiny sod house right here on the Circle Y!

"They needed a place to stay," said Momma. "They're family. We couldn't turn them away."

"Your momma has a big heart," said Caleb,

looking down at her with such love that Sadie blushed.

Momma frowned. "You said it was fine with you, Caleb."

"And it sure is." Caleb kissed Momma right on the lips. It didn't bother him that Sadie and Riley were standing right there watching.

"We can get used to havin' them here," said Riley. He knew he'd be out with the cattle most of the time anyway. He saw the look on Sadie's face, and he felt sorry for her. "Sadie, you can have Gerda help you pick up cow chips . . . And teach her how to hunt. I can see her out there now, shootin' the sky full of holes while she's tryin' to kill a rabbit." Riley's eyes twinkled, but he kept back the laugh he felt building inside.

Sadie wanted to scream at the top of her lungs the way Gerda did, but she knew that wouldn't be right. "Momma, do I have to wait on them?"

"You must be kind and thoughtful," said Momma.

"But you are not their slave," said Caleb firmly.

"But serve them as you would God," said Momma.

"But don't do things for them that they can do for themselves," said Caleb, tapping Momma's nose with his finger. "That goes for you too . . . not just the kids."

Momma sighed heavily. It was very hard for her to say no to company.

Her head spinning with what Momma and Caleb had said, Sadie brushed a strand of hair off her cheek. The warm wind pressed her skirts against her thin body. Finally she smiled. She'd stay as far away from Gerda as she could. She'd let

Opal deal with her. Besides, she had God to help her keep her temper and help her to be kind.

"We have good news too," said Caleb.

"What?" asked Sadie and Riley together.

"Sunday we're havin' a big celebration," Caleb said with a grin. "We sent word to our friends and neighbors to come for singin' and preachin' and celebratin'."

"Did you get the papers sayin' we're true Yorks?" asked Riley.

Sadie locked her fingers together and waited for Caleb's answer.

Caleb nodded. "But no more of that 'til Sunday."

Suddenly Sadie thought of something. "But how did you know we'd be back Sunday? . . . Or anytime?"

Caleb kissed Sadie's cheek. "Your momma, the kids, and I prayed for your safe return. I went off lookin' for you and didn't find you, but God is bigger than me. So we put Him to work lookin' for you to bring you back safe and sound . . . And He did it."

"We knew He would," said Momma.

"Now we want to hear all about your adventures," said Caleb with a quick glance toward the tiny sod house. "Tell us while you have a chance."

"After that you'll both take a bath," said Momma, wrinkling her nose at their smell.

Sadie laughed. She knew she smelled as bad as she looked. She gazed off across the prairie at the tiny dots that she knew were Opal, Web, Helen, and Tanner. Oh, but it was good to be home! She glanced at the tiny sod house. She would not let Gerda dim her happiness!

Caleb led the way to Momma's tree, and they

all sat in the shade while Sadie and Riley told Caleb and Momma all about the past several days.

That night Sadie lay in her bed with Helen in the middle and Opal on the far side. A cricket chirruped in the corner, and Riley snored from his bed on the other side of the sheeting. At the sound of Caleb's and Momma's soft voices Sadie smiled. For a while it had looked like she'd never sleep in her bed again, but here she was. "Thank You, Heavenly Father," she whispered.

14

A True York

Sunday morning Sadie waited near the well for Jewel Comstock and Mary Ferguson. Sadie smoothed down her good dress and touched her shiny, clean braids. She'd finished getting ready first so she'd have time to talk with Mary, her very best friend, before anyone else came. Jewel and Mary were near enough now that Sadie could see the team and wagon with Jewel's big black dog Malachi running alongside.

Just then Gerda walked up. Her ruffled green dress and bonnet looked brand-new. "Who's coming?" she asked.

Sadie had already told her a dozen times who would be coming today. "It's Jewel Comstock and Mary Ferguson."

"But a cow and a horse are pulling that wagon!"

"I know . . . Annie and Ernie. Jewel says they don't know they look strange together and not to tell them they do."

Gerda frowned. "That's silly." Gerda looked past the wagon. "Look, it's Levi!"

Sadie ignored the stab of jealousy.

"I only agreed to stay here in that horrible mud hut because of Levi," said Gerda with a toss of her head.

Suddenly Sadie could see right through Gerda. Gerda had had to stay no matter how much she stormed and cried because her parents had nowhere else to live until Mart earned some money. To her surprise, Sadie felt sorry for Gerda. "If you really want to impress Levi you should learn to ride and shoot," said Sadie. "I'll teach you . . . if you want."

Her eyes wide in shock, Gerda stared at Sadie. Warm wind tugged at her skirts and flipped the ends of her black hair. Then she smiled and lifted her chin. "I impress him just the way I am. But I might want to learn to ride and shoot just for something interesting to do while we're here."

"Anytime you're ready," said Sadie. By then Jewel was close enough that she called a loud howdy. Mary waved. Sadie ran to meet them while Gerda waited for Levi.

Later, with the others sitting nearby, Sadie stood beside Mary in the shade of Momma's tree and watched the Missouri family, the Hepfords, walk across the prairie playing guitar, fiddle, banjo, mouth organ, and hammered dulcimer. Sadie pressed her hands to her heart and listened. The music floated over her and around her, and she couldn't speak for the beauty of it. She watched the two bachelors from Cottonwood Creek ride in with a cloud of dust and saw the sudden spark of interest on Gerda's face. Joshua Cass came too, this time driving a wagon instead of riding a horse. Lost Sand Cherry and Good One rode on the seat with him. Sadie caught Mary's hand and squeezed it happily. She'd told Mary all about her Indian friends.

After introductions all around, singing, Bible reading, and prayer, Caleb stood before the group with his hat in his hands. Wind ruffled his buff-colored muslin shirt. Laugh lines spread from the corners of his blue eyes to the few gray hairs just above his dark sideburns. "This is a special day for me today, and I wanted all of you to share it." He caught Momma's hand, lifted her from her chair, and tugged her to stand with him. She flushed prettily, but held her head high. She wore her new bonnet and dress that she'd sewed from the blue calico the Missouri family had given them when Sadie taught Mitch Hepford how to cook and sew.

Sadie peeked at Riley beside her. He looked as nervous as she felt. Opal loved all the attention, and she was smiling her prettiest. Helen and Web could hardly stand still. They were ready to eat the food crowded on the long table, then play with Vard Hepford.

Caleb unfolded a paper he held in his hand. "All of you know I was on my own for a long time. I had no family. Then I married this beautiful lady, and her family became mine."

Tears stung Sadie's eyes, and she blinked them quickly away. She would not let anyone see her cry!

"This paper says that these young'uns now carry my name legal-like." Caleb drew Opal, Sadie, and Helen forward. "These are my daughters—Opal

125

Margaret York, Sadie Rose York, and Helen Irene York." He kissed them each, and the audience cheered.

Sadie's heart burst with things she wanted to say, but she stood quietly while Opal told Caleb they were proud to be his daughters.

Riley looped his thumbs in his belt and waited. He did want the York name, but he had been born a Merrill, and it didn't seem quite fair for Pa's name to be dropped. He had tried to tell Caleb how he felt, but he hadn't been able to find the words.

Caleb beckoned for Riley and Web. "These are my sons—Riley John Merrill York and Webster Jay Merrill York. Those are mighty big handles, but these men deserve them."

Riley choked back tears as he hugged Caleb, then let Web have a turn while everyone cheered and clapped.

After dinner Sadie leaned against the fence at the garden just to have a minute alone. Tomorrow she'd have to pick green beans. If it didn't rain they'd have to water the cucumbers. Pa had liked cucumbers better than anything else from the garden. Sadie smiled. She had loved Pa, but he had kept himself apart from them even when he sat in the same room. Caleb didn't do that. He laughed and talked and listened. Pa would want them to be happy.

"Sadie."

She turned around to find Levi walking toward her, his hand behind his back. Gerda was standing beside the house talking to the bachelors.

"Hi," Sadie said, smiling.

"I brought you a present for your special day."

Her heart jerked. "You did?"

"Pa said it was all right to bring it." Levi

brought his hand out from behind his back and held out the hat from Cotton's wagon that Sadie had admired so much. "This is for you."

Sadie's eyes filled, and she couldn't move. Finally she took the hat and set it on her head. It felt as wonderful as it had when she'd first tried it on. "Thank you," she whispered.

Levi shrugged. "I knew you liked it."

"I do, but I never thought I'd own it."

"Pa says he has to put a notice in the paper to see if Cotton Twyll owed anybody money before he can do anything with the rest of the stuff, but he let me bring this to you."

"I love it, Levi!" She touched the brim. "I don't think I'll ever take it off." She laughed, and so did Levi. It felt like old times.

Levi leaned against the fence beside Sadie. "Pa said Good One could stay with us. He might take over the peddler's wagon."

"That's nice."

Levi was quiet a long time. "Sadie?"

"Yes?"

"I hope we can always be friends, no matter how Gerda acts around me."

Sadie smiled. She'd already dealt with that. "We can."

Levi grinned. "Good."

Sadie glanced over Levi's shoulder and saw Good One looking at her. "I have to go now. Good One, Mitch Hepford, and I are going to have a footrace. The one who wins gets the new bullwhip the bachelors brought . . . And I intend to win!"

"I hope you do," said Levi with a grin.

Sadie ran to get in line with Good One and Mitch. She knew even if she lost the race she'd still be the happiest girl in all of Nebraska. She was

Sadie Rose York, a true York! And she had a hat that suited her.

She smiled at Good One, then at Mitch. "Ready when you are," she said.